Tempered Steel

Vikings of Honor, Book Four

RENEE
VINCENT

TEMPERED STEEL
Copyright © 2017, Renee Vincent
Trade Paperback ISBN: 9781944484125

Digital ISBN: 9781944484118
Hardback ISBN: 9781944484187

Cover Art Design by Renee Vincent
Stock Art by BigStock.com
Editor, Linda Ingmanson
Digital Release: July, 2017
Trade Paperback Release: July, 2017
Hardback Release: March, 2022

Publishing History
Originally published by Turquoise Morning Press under the title *The Temperate Warrior*, Copyright © 2012 by Renee Vincent

First Edition of revised work published by Renee Vincent under the title *The Temperate Warrior*, Copyright © 2015 by Renee Vincent

For God, who is my strength and my constant companion.

For those who love to read historical romance novels.

Praise for TEMPERED STEEL

"Heartwarming, heart pounding, and spellbinding!
I cannot find fault in this author's work as she weaves
each enchanting tale."
—*Night Owl Reviews*

"An action-packed tale, I could not put down, staying
up late into the night to finish it. Brimming with
humor, passion, complex and compelling characters,
an intriguing plot, witty repartee, suspense, danger, and
a one-of-a-kind love. This beautifully written story is
delicious. A definite keeper!"
—*Romance Junkies*

"Vincent writes well and has obviously done her
research to accurately describe the culture of the
Norsemen. You'll enjoy this well written
continuation."
**—Award-winning historical fiction author,
Regan Walker**

"It's the perfect conclusion for her beautiful Viking
series. Well written and researched details of the Viking

world make this book a must to read! I highly recommend her 4 books in the Vikings of Honor series!"
—N. Laverdure, Book Reviewer

"Nobody writes a Viking love story incomparable in steam and unrestrained temperance like Renee Vincent. This equals Daegan's passionate beginning in *Sunset Fire* (book I) without the heartbreaking end of it (thank the gods). Vincent's writing pulls in a passionate reader. Her bite is strong."
—(Ashleys) Amazon Book Reviewer

TEMPERED STEEL
Vikings of Honor, Book 4

Gustaf Ræliksen lives by the blade of his sword. After avenging his father's murder and reuniting with his family, he wants nothing more than to settle down and have sons of his own. Only one woman will do—a beautiful redheaded *thrall* he saved from the spoils of war.

Free from slavery and those who kept her captive, Æsa has nothing to offer the noble warrior except her heart. But when someone with a deep score to settle seeks revenge and the whereabouts of buried silver that only Æsa knows, she must break Gustaf's heart in order to spare his life.

Gustaf's world is torn asunder, and he has but one vow— saving the woman he loves from the dangerous rival who will stop at nothing to have it all.

***Previously published as *The Temperate Warrior.* (This new edition has been partially rewritten and professionally edited, along with a new title and new cover.)

Chapter One

Gustaf Ræliksen crumpled the pretty embroidered cloth in his fist and brought it to his nose, breathing in the lingering scent of lavender and primrose one last time before tucking it back inside the sleeve of his kirtle. He looked out over the calm, deep blue water as he approached the Orkneys, torn between steering his longship toward the Faroe Islands or sailing eastward toward Skíringssalr. On the Faroes waited the woman he hadn't seen in over a month—his dearest Æsa. In Skíringssalr waited the families of his loyal men who hadn't seen them in over twenty-three years.

Gustaf and his men had been scouring the known world for ten spineless cowards hired by King Harald the Fairhair, who had killed his father. Though the handful of murderers were anything but stealthy, they certainly knew how to make themselves scarce, often taking refuge in places unfit for humans. Lands so cold and barren, only a marked man would dare to go. Desperation did that to a man, especially when one knew a dreadful fate awaited. And no one in his right mind would have wanted to die in the manner Gustaf deemed necessary. His father had been hung from the rafters in his barn by his own intestines, and nothing less had been dealt forth toward his foes.

From the time he left home to avenge his father at the age of nineteen, Gustaf had not stopped until every last one of them had been found and left to die in the same agonizing manner. However, if not for his seven *hirdmen* aboard the vessel, he would not have been able to fulfill his duty as a loyal son. It was because of their dedication to his cause that he made haste to reunite his steadfast friends with their families now. It was the least he could do for their undaunted devotion and service.

Even still, his heart ached to throw duty overboard and storm up the east coast of Skúvoy, seeking out the owner of the kerchief in his possession. He'd been fortunate enough to find Æsa when he barged into the longhouse of one of his father's murderers a few months prior. She was a slave to Ragnar, son of Thorrstein, at the time Gustaf had given him a chance to offer up the last coward's name in exchange for a swift death. Ragnar refused and, thus, his gruesome fate had been handed to him without delay.

Though Gustaf had not gained a name, he hadn't left empty-handed. He'd taken the shapely young redhead from the dead man's possession. As he saw it, a dead man had no need for a beautiful woman in his bed.

Gustaf had claimed her for his own and his equal, making it very clear he'd never share her with another man. She'd promised her bed to no one but him, and he believed her. Perhaps he'd been a fool to do so, but he couldn't help it.

During the few weeks he'd spent with her in a deserted cottage along the outskirts of the small settlement of Skúvoy, she'd given him no reason to deem otherwise. The conversations they'd fallen into and the intimate moments they'd shared, warmed by a crackling fire, were things he'd never freely shared with anyone, save her. By rights, she should have been sickened by the wicked brutality of his past, but it seemed she'd uncovered the real man behind the mail armor and leather.

By the time they'd parted ways, a temporary separation so that Gustaf could kill the last known man who'd murdered his father, she knew everything about him and never shied from his touch. With willing, delicate hands, she'd held him close and whispered sweet promises in his ear before he'd left. *"I'll be here when you return, Gustaf. No matter how long you're absent from my arms, you'll find me here, waiting."*

Gustaf took a deep breath of the crisp sea air, trying to push aside his longing for the woman he so missed. He glanced one last time at the islands behind him and made a silent vow that he would return for her as soon as he could.

Affirming his grip on the steer board, he looked ahead and dutifully stayed the course toward his men's homeland. The wind had picked up on the open sea, and the need for rowing had diminished.

Several of his men had resorted to keeping themselves busy within the hull of the ship. A few sharpened daggers; a couple more quietly discussed the simple pleasures they missed and which ones they planned to treat themselves to first. But Jørgen, his closest friend, looked as if he were fighting boredom. Gustaf noticed he'd been eyeing him ever since they'd hoisted the heavy pine mast into its chink hole and rigged the single woolen sail against it.

Jørgen finally arose from his rowing bench and approached Gustaf at the stern. "Permission to speak, my lord."

Gustaf smiled. "Your service to me ended the moment Gunnar Haveloksen took his last breath. There is no need to address me as your master. You're free to speak to your heart's content, my friend."

An air of haughtiness seemed to have overtaken Jørgen. "Noting your request, I demand you turn this *langskip* around."

Gustaf regarded his friend's statement carefully. "And why would I do that?"

"I'm not a fool," Jørgen replied. "I've seen the magnitude of your yearning for the woman you've left behind. If not for this burden of sailing us homeward, you would've already burst through her door."

"If not for *you*, I wouldn't have a woman to come home to at all."

"Indeed," Jørgen admitted. "But 'tis not fair to put your men before yourself. You've been more than generous to us. Not only with payment for our services but for the sacrifices you've made on our behalf."

"I assure you, my sacrifices pale in comparison to the ones you and the others have made for me. I'll not ask any of you to give up more. You've been kept from your families far longer than I care to admit, and I'll not coerce you to wait longer."

"What you say is true. We have been without the comfort of our families, the embraces of our children while they were small, and the warmth of our women in our beds. Some of us aren't so certain we have women at all. Through the years, it has felt as if forever has passed since we've taken in those simple joys. We have withstood eternity without them. What is one more day?"

Gustaf felt his resolve slip. For a split second, Jørgen's offer tempted him to steer the ship southward and disregard his sense of duty. He then shook his head. "One more day is one more too long. If I could steal control of the wind from the gods, I would've already dragged keel in Skíringssalr by now, and we'd not be having this discussion."

"If you could steal any power from the gods, my lord, I doubt it would be something as frivolous as the wind. I'd imagine you would have robbed Thor of his hammer and destroyed your father's murderers single-handedly with one swift blow. Then none of us would've been slave to this bloody ship."

Gustaf laughed as he pondered the thought of wielding Mjollnir for the sake of time and effort. "Wish I would've thought of that twenty-three years ago when I was praying to the gods."

Jørgen glanced over his shoulder at the eager men who grew intent at the conversation at hand. He squared his shoulders and looked Gustaf in the eye. "Through those many years we've spent together, are we not your brothers?"

"Of course you are."

"Then as your brother, I cannot bear the thought of saying our farewells in haste. It would not feel right in my heart to step off this vessel and watch you leave us behind like cargo of little importance. Reuniting with my family wouldn't be the same if you weren't there to share in my joy. I'm asking for you to spend a few days with us before you set sail for Inishmore. Please, I beg you. Turn this *langskip* around and bring Æsa with us. At first light, tomorrow morn, we can sail for Skíringssalr together."

Gustaf clasped Jørgen's shoulder. "Speak no more, my brother. I hadn't given thought to what parting with you would mean." Gustaf extended his hand, gesturing toward his entire crew. "Or what 'twould be like without all of you at my side. My mind hadn't wandered outside of being buried in Æsa's embrace, it seems. I'm a man. Can you blame me?"

Hearty chuckles collected within the hull, and it felt good to hear his men laugh.

"Does this mean you'll accept my offer?" Jørgen asked.

Gustaf's heart skipped a beat as he thought of seeing his dearest Æsa this day. "Lower the mast and take command of your oars. We sail for Skúvoy."

Chapter Two

Æsa stepped into the brisk afternoon air. As the cool breeze met her face, she breathed in the fresh sea salt coming off the North Atlantic. It was mid-autumn, and she knew winter would soon nip at its heels. With each passing day, she worried over Gustaf's safety and spent many hours gazing out over the ocean for signs of his return.

Counting the days by the cycle of the moon, she determined he'd been gone for over a month. It had been the longest stretch of time without his comforting presence. From the moment he'd left to save his family from Gunnar Haveloksen, she'd been lost without him.

She recalled the short weeks she'd spent with Gustaf after he rescued her from the callous hands of Ragnar. He'd known the disgraceful life she'd lived of warming countless men's beds in exchange for food or shelter. It was a life she'd not chosen willingly. Ripped from her homeland in Norway, she'd been thrust into the slave market at the age of four and ten when her family had been slaughtered at Harald Fairhair's command. Gustaf had known all this, but still he took her in and showed her nothing but kindness. He'd treated her as an equal, insisting she'd never be a slave to any man again, including himself. Choosing of her own free will, she'd stayed with Gustaf and found more happiness than she'd ever dreamed possible.

Beneath his tender touch, Æsa quickly learned it was possible for a woman to enjoy the pleasures of the flesh. Not to fear the approach of a man's naked body, but glory in its raw beauty. Through him, she'd learned what a real man was, and because of him, she'd discovered a sense of worth, a virtue no man had ever offered. Those simple deeds helped her realize that not all men were vermin, spawn of Loki.

Gustaf was an honest man who spoke only the truth. When he'd promised to return for her, she held his vow close to her heart. She'd wait forever if need be.

Only a month in, her wait had already felt like forever. She couldn't get used to Gustaf's absence. She'd thought after being forced to share her bed for so long that she'd welcome the temporary respite from a man's inexorable sexual desires. But since the first night she'd spent with Gustaf, she became accustomed to the delights of his feral appetite. His craving for flesh upon flesh had grown to be hers, and every night that passed without his embrace left her feeling deserted and lonely.

She'd never felt these emotions before. In the past, as she'd lain listening to the snores of men, she dreamed of slitting their throats with their own daggers. Or, at the least, castrating them for all the despicable things they'd required of her. Oh, the number of ways she plotted their deaths…

Since Gustaf, that kind of hatred had left her. Only passion and joy filled her heart, and now the feeling of missing him so greatly, it hurt. To her, waiting for her beloved Gustaf was more painful than any hardship she'd endured from her past.

Many times, she prayed to both Thor and the All-father, Odin, to aid in Gustaf's return, hoping that one morning she'd discover his *langskip* drifting ashore on the distant banks of the Faroes. And each day, her pleas seemed to go unheard.

From her viewpoint atop the lush green hill that sat below the mountain of Knúkur, she could see the grassy rooftops of the many houses below. Like her, the inhabitants of the isle had escaped the torments of Harald Fairhair and lived here in relative peace. No one bothered her as she dwelled in solitude, lest they face the wrath of Gustaf Ræliksen. She had come to learn that his reputation as a deadly swordsman was known far and wide, and any man would be a fool to try his hand at besting Gustaf's skills.

The only man who dared to venture up the hillock was an old warrior named Didrik. Gustaf had assured her he was a trustworthy friend of many years and would check on her weekly. Though Didrik bore the likeness of a disreputable character with his warily shifting eyes and scruffy bearded face, she had come to enjoy his visits. Along with the pleasant conversation about his late wife and his two adventure-seeking sons, he often brought fresh cow's milk and *skerpikjøt*. Though the chewy meat was unlike anything she'd ever eaten, it was certainly a treat for her empty belly.

As Æsa gathered her cloak more tightly beneath her chin, she picked up a wooden pail near the entrance of the cottage to gather water from a nearby stream and noticed a group of men hiking up the hill. Knowing Didrik wasn't due for another couple of days, she hoped it was Gustaf and his men returning. There was just the right number of men, but something didn't sit right with Æsa. They were fully armored with helmets and shields as they bypassed the cluster of homes below and marched up the steep incline. The sheer determination in their steps resembled raiding Northmen set on plunder rather than the return of her warrior lover and his men.

Her heart sank, and the bucket in her grasp dropped to the ground. Stark, cold fear pierced her body like shards of ice. She had witnessed the carnage left behind by these kinds of raids a thousand times over. It was because of this cruelty that her days as a whore had begun. And now that she was free, she wasn't about to go back. She'd die before she'd let another man force himself upon her.

Æsa turned on her heel and darted back inside, her only thoughts of Gustaf and making sure not one of them made it atop the hill alive.

Chapter Three

Gustaf cocked his head, confused by the sound of the distant slamming door. He'd thought as soon as Æsa saw him, she would have run like mad for him. Instead, she turned away and clapped the door shut.

He stopped in his tracks, and his men did the same. He felt the weight of their stares almost as much as he bore the disappointment of Æsa's reaction to his return.

"My lord?" Jørgen asked.

Gustaf gazed at his friend for a moment and then back toward the house on the hill. "Perhaps she wishes not to see me. Was I foolish to believe the promise of a woman?"

"In my experience," Jørgen offered, "the solidity of a woman's oath is often stronger than that of a man's. Forgive me for prying, but did you leave her in a state of anger?"

Gustaf shook his head. "On the contrary, we parted with a kiss. She vowed she'd wait for me." He recalled the softness of Æsa's touch upon his face and the sincerity of her words. He knew she had plenty of practice at wooing men, but he assumed she'd not stoop to manipulating him. Mayhap he'd been a fool like all the rest.

"Then I'm certain she waits for you," Jørgen tried to reason. "Albeit…behind closed doors."

Gustaf gave him a sideways glance, unimpressed with his friend's jest. He swallowed the hard lump of humiliation and blew out a forceful sigh. "Those of you who've taken a wife, step forward."

Out of the seven, only three took the stride forward. One by one, Gustaf looked at each man in desperation. "In the realm of weaponry and warfare, I'm a practiced man. I can outwit any opponent who dares to confront me. This you all know well. But, for the love of Odin, will someone please school me in the schemes of the female kind?"

Before any of the men could voice their knowledge, an arrow pierced the ground at Gustaf's feet. Immediately, everyone dropped to their knees and hid behind the safety of their shields, including Gustaf.

Snorri, one of his men who'd never taken a wife, piped up with a possible explanation. "With all due respect, my lord, there be no scheming here, for without a doubt, your woman is trying to kill you."

Gustaf glared at him. "Is that so?"

"Either that or she's lost the sight in her eyes and thinks you to be a red stag sure to feed her stomach this winter."

Gustaf glanced down at the thick gray wolf fur across his shoulders. She would have to be colorblind to mistake his wolf-skin cloak for a deer's hide. In seeing the ridiculous smile on Snorri's lips, he scolded himself for even listening to his friend. Instead, he looked to Jørgen for a better reason, but to his surprise, his friend possessed the same irreverent smile as Snorri. "You too find humor in this?"

"My apologies, my lord. But aye, I do."

Gustaf growled and peeked over the rim of his shield, catching a glimpse of Æsa taking aim. Ducking back down, he felt the arrow hit its mark in his wooden shield. He grimaced and tucked himself more tightly behind the shield. "Has she gone mad?"

After an outburst of laughter, Jørgen cleared his throat as if trying to gain his composure. "Perhaps in your excitement to see her, you've neglected the obvious. My guess is she knows not who beckons her." He tapped his helmet upon his head. "You look like every other Northman who aims to take his spoils."

The obvious flooded Gustaf's brain. How could he be so slow of mind? Before he'd left, he instructed her to do whatever necessary to stay alive. And if anyone dared to venture past the harbor, save for Didrik, he'd demanded she protect herself at all costs. He had even lent his dagger should she need it.

He was pleased she took his orders to protect herself so seriously, but where had she acquired the bow and the skills to use it?

Another arrow whizzed past, slicing between him and Jørgen. Though Gustaf knew he had to find a way to let Æsa know it was he, the last thing he wanted to do was remove the protective helmet from the top half of his face and head.

"Give me an arrow," he demanded.

Jørgen's eyes widened in shock. "My lord?"

"Do it!"

Obediently, Jørgen reached over his shoulder into his quiver and tossed an arrow to his chieftain. Gustaf dug into his sleeve and pulled out the embroidered piece of cloth, then tied it to the arrow just behind the blade. He pitched it back to his friend and said, "Wait for my signal before firing."

Jørgen's mouth fell agape. "Surely you don't wish me to kill her?"

"Be not so dim of wit," Gustaf scolded. "Shoot the arrow in the ground beside her so she knows 'tis I who have come for her. And you best not miss your mark, or I shall have to kill *you*."

Jørgen smiled uneasily and readied himself with his bow. He kept his eyes on Gustaf, waiting for his command. As a fourth arrow careened past, Gustaf gave the word and Jørgen stood up. With only seconds to spare, he pulled back his bow and let it fly before dropping to the ground and righting his shield in front of him.

With bated breath, Gustaf waited. As the moments ticked by, he clenched his jaw. "Tell me you didn't miss."

"Of course I didn't."

Impatience got the best of Gustaf. "What is she doing?"

"How would I know, my lord?" Jørgen said in

irritation. "I'm crouched behind my shield as you are. Why do you not look for yourself?"

Gustaf growled and tentatively lifted his head above his shield. He saw Æsa pluck the arrow from the ground at her feet and inspect the cloth. She glanced down the hillock, and he hesitantly stood to wave. He thought he heard a squeal as she brought both hands to her mouth, then glanced at Jørgen, who had also begun to stand. "Is that a sound I should be wary of?"

Jørgen laughed. "Not unless you fear the prospect of a woman leaping into your arms," he concluded, pointing.

Gustaf looked back at Æsa, who was now running down the hill, her smiling face beaming with joy and relief.

****

Æsa could not believe her eyes as she flew to get to Gustaf. A million thoughts raced through her mind, each one swiftly on the heels of the next, matching the speed of her stumbling feet. While her heart leapt, she couldn't believe she'd rained down a multitude of arrows set on killing him. But by the look on his face, Gustaf didn't seem to mind that she had threatened his life. His arms were open and ready to enfold her the moment she met his embrace.

In a few strides, she closed the distance between them and slammed into his chest, her arms wrapping like a vise around his neck. Gustaf hardly staggered from the brunt of the blow. His thick, burly body halted the force of her momentum and his arms gathered her up in a lively spin. Though he made not a sound, she felt his utter joy through the compelling strength of his grasp and the endearing way he breathed in her scent. She relished this moment, content to remain in his arms forever.

"You waited for me," he whispered against her neck. His soft lips, warm breath, and prickly beard brushed across her skin and goose-pimpled her flesh. As profound as those words were upon her senses, they weren't audible enough for his men to hear. She tightened her arms around him and replied in the same covert manner. "Of course, I did. I promised I would. Did you have your doubts?"

Gustaf squeezed her one more time before setting her to her feet. He lifted his shield from the ground and yanked the arrow that had lodged itself in the wood. "I believed you up until the first of these were cast."

Æsa hid her guilt beneath a downward glance. "Forgive me. I meant no harm to you and your men. I thought—"

He lifted her chin with a strong hand and smiled. "We all stand before you unscathed." He then threw his men a stern look. "Is that not right?"

Collectively, the seven agreed and nodded happily to please their chieftain. Æsa smiled in return, thankful that she hadn't been skillful with the bow her first time. She hated to think what could have happened.

Instead, she gathered her wits, and invited the men to

follow her up the hill to the little stone cottage Gustaf had set her up in, talking as she led the way. "I regret to admit I haven't lit a fire within the hearth, nor have I prepared any food for the day, but the thick stone walls and grassy roof will block this constant wind. Of that, you can be sure. 'Course, you all being men, you might not even mind it. I didn't mind it. The howl of the breeze puts me to sleep every night. 'Tis the fog I can't seem to get used to. Very thick. And eerie."

Gustaf caught up with her and halted her by the elbow. "Why is it you haven't any food for the day? Had I not bestowed enough silver in your keeping?"

She didn't want him to think he'd not been generous, but she stumbled on her explanation. "You left me with more than enough, m'lord, but I was not certain how long 'twould last should you be delayed because of winter. I lived on necessity, spending your reserves only when my strength of body and mind begged for it."

In all honesty, there was probably enough there to last her more than two winters, but given her lack of experience with living a life of luxury, she hadn't squandered a single ounce of it simply because it was available.

Gustaf looked her up and down as if gauging the amount of weight she'd lost since he last saw her. "Jørgen," he commanded, never averting his eyes from her.

"My lord?" his friend answered, stepping forward.

"Take the men down to the shore and fish. Do not return until there is enough to fill each of our stomachs with two."

Æsa tried to interject, but Gustaf raised his hand and silenced her. "Better yet, make certain my Æsa has three."

As the men did as they were told without complaint, Jørgen turned and muttered a suggestive question in his chieftain's ear. "And what will you do, my lord?"

Gustaf peeled his gaze from Æsa and regarded Jørgen from the corner of his eye. "I shall stoke a fire."

Jørgen scoffed and landed a hard pat on Gustaf's back. "I wager the fire you aim to set will not cook a single fish."

Chapter Four

Æsa felt the burden of Gustaf's stare burning a hole in her back as they trekked up the remainder of the hill. Even after they reached the security of the cottage, she felt the relentless heat of his gaze.

She ushered Gustaf inside, then quickly approached the cold, smoky hearth in the center of the room in order to relight a fire. Unable to face him, she stared at the logs of peat. "I've angered you."

"If I were angry, you'd know it."

She closed her eyes and drew in a breath of courage. Never in all her days of pleasing men had she cared what they thought. Oftentimes, she'd speak ill on purpose so they'd grow tired of her disdainful tongue and pass her on to someone else. But with Gustaf, she couldn't help but want to gratify his every whim.

When she revealed she hadn't used the silver he'd given her to live on, she noticed the discontentment that continued to crease his brow. To a degree, she'd insulted him. "If I've not angered you, then I've surely made you feel less of a man in front of your warriors."

Gustaf's hearty scoff caused her to turn her head in his

direction. "Is that what you think?" he asked, drawing near.

The twinkle of gaiety lighting his blue eyes confused her. If he wasn't angry with her, and he wasn't humiliated, then what was he? She froze within her thin leather shoes, stiffening at his proximity. He reached for her wrist and pulled her into his arms. "Only if you were gone from this earth would I be less of a man."

His tender words took her by surprise. They were heartfelt and sincere, quite different from the clipped statements he'd made a few moments before. She was not used to a man's mood swinging like a pendulum from one extreme to the next. It was difficult to keep up.

He playfully nipped at her nose and backed her against the vertical beam of the room. "I've missed you."

Sandwiched between the dense face of the wood and the solid wall of his chest, she valued the dominance of his character but was still unsure of his ever-changing demeanor. He expressed authority and power by means of a mighty body and challenging eyes, yet behind that brawny exterior seemed to lie a man as gentle as the tender reeds swaying along the marshes.

Tentatively, she placed her hands on his chest and stroked him around his shoulders, lacing her fingers behind his neck. She considered a nickname that had come to her amid his embrace, and decided to test it upon Gustaf himself. "And I have missed you, my temperate warrior."

He quirked a solitary brow. "You do realize your pet name does little to describe the fierceness I would rather be remembered for?"

She rubbed noses with him and relished the feel of his body pressed against hers. "Far be it from me to defame your fierce reputation among men, but 'tis not violent hostility I remember in these hands…these eyes…these lips…"

Gustaf captured hers in a hard, demanding kiss the moment she spoke of them. The soft wet heat of his mouth had her gasping in surprise and buckling at the knees. She tightened her arms around his neck and hoisted her legs around his waist. Large hands cupped her bottom as he positioned her over his thick erection.

A low groan escaped him as if a multitude of sensations racked his body. He spun her from the beam and broke away from the kiss, his eyes boring into hers. "I should build that fire I promised before I lose all might for such a simple task." He then allowed her body to slide ever so slowly down the length of him before setting her on her feet.

Æsa brushed her hands down her tunic, adjusted her clothes, and tucked a strand of hair behind her ear. If Gustaf hadn't stopped when he had, there was no telling how far her own passion would've taken her.

She forced herself to think of other things besides Gustaf's hard body that she missed so much. Things that pertained to the very reason he left her behind to begin with and the questions she had about the month she'd spent separated from him. With his return, did that mean they had successfully avenged his father and saved his family from Gunnar Havloksen's deceit? Was his family alive and well? Were they happy to see him after all these years?

No sooner had she brought to mind his family, she realized Gustaf had to have left them behind a second time in order to come back for her. At first, it seemed admirable of him to do such a thing, but then she felt guilty for putting him in a position where he had to choose between her and his family. Given the years he'd spent and the lengths to which he'd gone to avenge his father, there was no denying how devoted Gustaf could be to a cause. Once he said it would be done, he'd keep his word or die trying. Perhaps his word to return for her was simply to uphold a promise. A vow of duty rather than love.

"You've lost words for speaking all of a sudden," Gustaf said, breaking the silence. "Are you not happy to see me?"

Æsa busied herself by reaching into the rafters for the herbs she'd hung for drying and fiddled with the knot tied around the stems. "I'm very happy to see you, my lord. You mistake my silence for displeasure."

He blew gently on the tiny sparks grasping at the bundles of kindling he arranged in the hearth. His eyes remained fixed on hers. "I cannot read your thoughts any more than you can mine, Æsa. Speak to me so that I may know what troubles you."

"There are no words to describe how my heart is

feeling. But you should know that I'm relieved by your return."

He stood from the slow-burning fire of turf, and the smoke trailed upward beside him. "You're surprised I've come back for you."

She tried to let her spinning emotions settle before answering. The solemnity and confusion projecting from his gaze warned her to speak carefully. The last thing she wanted was to anger Gustaf with her insecurities. Nervously, she bit her lip. "I'm surprised you've come back for someone who's unworthy of your return." She swallowed against the harsh dryness in her throat. "A man like you deserves a more noble woman than I. You're the eldest son of a chieftain, the pride of your family."

"And you're the daughter of a brave warrior, a perfect match in my eyes."

"You didn't know my father," Æsa reminded him. "So, you can't make that claim."

"Nay, I was denied that privilege. But in knowing you, do I see him. I imagine he was a loving father and a courageous fighter who, for the sake of his family, would not give up the fight against his enemies. He died trying to save you and your mother. There is no greater love than that."

"What you say about my father is true, but I've shamed him. Just as I shame you now."

"Look at me, Æsa," he demanded. "Look into my eyes and tell me if you see shame."

She could barely do so. "A cunning man knows how to hide it. I would be a fool to think you're not ashamed that I was once a whore."

From the corner of her eye, she saw Gustaf cringe upon hearing that word, and his brow furrowed deeply across his forehead. "A slave to that life, you are no longer. In my presence, you'll not utter that dreadful word ever again. Do you understand?"

Æsa pinched off one of the seeds from the dried bundle of herbs in her hands and nodded.

Gustaf came to her in two quick strides, snatching the herbs from her grasp and tossing them on the boxbed. He gathered her hands and brought her knuckles to his lips. He planted a kiss upon each and stared longingly into her eyes. "You've brought many things into my life, all of which have made me a happier man than I could ever imagine. But never shame." She turned her head away, but he reached for her chin, directing it upward to face him. "Never shame," he reiterated sternly. "Tell me you believe in what I say, for I cannot continue to love you if you think my every word is a lie."

Æsa's heart tripped on the string of endearments that fell from Gustaf's mouth. *Continue to love you*, echoed in her head.

"Say you believe me," he commanded, pulling her into the cage of his arms.

She peered into his eyes and saw a blazing honesty within them. "You love me?"

The strength of his embrace weakened around her, and the hard lines around his eyes softened. "I came back for you, did I not?"

Disappointment undulated through her. "Even a bird returns to its native land when winter passes. 'Tis not for love—"

"'Tis the reason I've returned."

Æsa felt nauseous and weak. She hadn't meant to put her all her hopes in one basket, but his reason for returning still sounded more like duty to her ears. She moved to escape him, and he tightened his grip around her back.

"Let go of me," she said sternly.

He shook his head. "I'm not letting go."

Her survival instincts kicked in, and she smacked him across the face. "Unhand me." She braced her hands on his chest and shoved.

He grabbed both her wrists and backed her against the nearest wall. Something ignited inside her, and she fought against being pinned. Her struggle proved futile, for he was stronger and more skillful at hand-to-hand combat in close quarters.

Fighting against the last attempts she made to wriggle free, he growled, "I'm not letting go of the woman I love. You'll hear me first, then I'll release you. Not a moment before."

Gustaf gave Æsa time to surrender, and a forceful sigh

declared her defeat. The flaming temper of his redheaded beauty delighted him beyond words. It was the first thing he'd liked about her when he and his men had burst into Ragnar's home. He remembered the sharp sound of her hand slapping Ragnar's face when Ragnar dismissed and insulted her in the same breath. She was a woman who could hold her own and wasn't afraid to make a stand, even if it resulted in physical pain.

He smiled when she averted her gaze, thankful that he'd finally awakened her fiery spirit. "You're such a stubborn woman. If you knew how much it charmed me, you wouldn't be so obstinate."

Her light eyes flared to heated embers as she glowered at some distant spot in the room. He'd seen that look before, but it had been with Ragnar. Today, the daggers were for him. As he confined her against the wall, he also noticed a fine sheen of perspiration on her skin. He could smell the redolence of oils coming from the pulse points of her neck while feeling the rapid rise and fall of her chest against his. Even in her angered state, she was the most gorgeous woman he'd ever seen.

"Do you remember the first time we were together, alone?" he asked.

Æsa closed her eyes. "Of course."

"Then you should also remember how much I gave you. I offered all of myself to you without expecting a single thing in return."

"I know."

"Realize, my dear Æsa, 'twas not out of duty. And this day is no different. I came back for you for one reason. For love."

A tear trailed down her cheek from behind her closed lids. The fire in her spirit was fizzling out.

"Look at me," he whispered.

When she opened her eyes and turned her head to face him, he saw the very reason he adored this temperamental woman who'd bewitched him months ago. Though life's cruelty had thieved every ounce of her self-worth, it hadn't stolen her tender heart.

He let go of her wrists, fearing he might have already bruised her beautiful alabaster skin, and brushed his thumb across her cheek. He wiped away the tear and looked her straight in the eye. "I'm without burden now. I've fulfilled my duty as a loyal son, and I've found my family. I'm at peace knowing my days of vengeance are behind me. I can start my life anew." He held her gaze for some time, allowing his words to sink in before continuing. "You're the only woman I want. There is no other who can light my lips with a smile, fill my heart with joy, and gratify my soul with pride. Marry me, Æsa, and let me spend the rest of my days doing the same for you." He cupped her face and tenderly kissed her trembling bottom lip. "Marry me."

Chapter Five

Æsa quivered beneath Gustaf's caress. His fingertips roamed the delicate skin of her face, erasing the trace of each new tear that fell. He answered every question she'd ever dared to ask and erased all the skeptical thoughts she'd had about his honorable intentions. She'd never doubt him again.

"Aye, my lord. I will marry you," she replied.

Gustaf smiled, and his blue eyes danced with delight. He pulled her into another kiss and lifted her off the floor. She felt weightless in his embrace, laughing with him as he spun her around.

This was the happiest day of her life, second only to the moment Gustaf burst through Ragnar's door and liberated her from the degrading life she'd been forced to live all those years. He was her savior in so many ways, and now, he'd soon be her husband. Nothing mattered to her save the day they'd be united in love. Waiting until that joyous day would be the hardest of all.

She closed her eyes and buried her nose in the safe haven of Gustaf's neck, savoring his masculine scent. She never believed she'd know true love in her lifetime, and she pinched her forearm just to be certain she wasn't dreaming. She felt the sting as sure as she felt his burly arms around her body.

While hugging him around the neck, she saw the embroidered cloth she'd untied from the shaft of Jørgen's arrow and tucked into her sleeve. She remembered how she'd originally given it to Gustaf before he left, and the look of pride in his eyes as he examined the colorful stitches that embellished the edges.

She pulled it free and brought it close to her heart. Slowly, Gustaf set her on her feet, and he too regarded the cloth in her hand. She looked up and saw the pride, once again, twinkling in his eyes.

Taking hold of his wrist, she lay the cloth in his palm and closed his fingers around it. "'Tis not much, but I've naught else to give you. Let this be a token of my love."

He brought his other hand over hers and bowed. "Of all the gifts bestowed unto me, this is the one I treasure most. 'Twas made by your hands and given to me from your heart. I'll cherish it always. And soon we'll stand before my family and proclaim our love before a multitude of witnesses. After that, I want to fill our home with many sons."

"And daughters?" she included gleefully.

"Aye, and daughters. I can only hope they resemble your beauty and speak with fire on their tongues."

"And if they do not?"

"I shall love them anyway," he proclaimed, "for they'll

come from your womb." He reverently touched her stomach. "Our children."

His eyes turned dark and his touch less innocent. Her desire for Gustaf yet again escalated, and his devious grin indicated that he also had urges of his own that needed satiating.

"Come with me," he said, taking her by the hand and tugging her out the door.

"Where are we going?"

"I need a bath, and you'll help me."

"What about your men? I don't want to be bathing when they return."

"Make no mistake, my men are skilled hunters and warriors. No living creature is safe where sword, spear, or bow are concerned. But when the task of fishing is in their hands, the slippery gilled beasts are more cunning. My men will not return for quite some time, this I know."

Æsa didn't argue with him as he led her from the longhouse and behind the small barn where a babbling clear stream cut through the hill. It was far too shallow for completely submerging oneself if standing, but it was pleasantly waist high in one particular spot.

She'd bathed at this waterhole many times but never lingered. She rarely felt safe enough on the isle to strip naked for longer than necessary, especially without a trustworthy lookout. Not to mention that the water was far too brisk this time of year to loiter in it. Judging by the look on Gustaf's face and the determination of his pace, he didn't seem concerned with either.

She watched him as he removed his belt and armor, and her heart picked up speed at the thought of seeing his beautiful, naked body. Admittedly, she'd longed for this moment for weeks, imagining his muscled form standing in the warm glow of the central hearth before he'd slip into the boxbed beside her.

She glanced around and checked their remote surroundings with a wary eye, and Gustaf had already peeled his boots and clothes from his body. He stood at the water's edge, naked as the day he was born, and dipped a toe beneath the surface. Æsa stood in awe, admiring the man who, for the first time in his life, hadn't a care in the world.

Under the afternoon sky, his legs were long and powerful from years of carrying a warrior's body across steep mountains and snow-drifted valleys. Dusted with golden hair, his skin was tan, smooth, and unmarred, save for a few scars across his wide back. In no way did the old battle wounds tarnish his manly appeal. If anything, the marks reminded her of the kind of man he was and how much he'd willingly endured to uphold his family's honor. From the blemishes carved into his skin, to the gentle, compassionate heart beating in his chest, Gustaf was the definition of noble.

Slowly, he walked into the water. The rippling stream rushed past his ankles and eventually over his knees as he strolled farther out. When it rose above his waist, he looked over his shoulder. "'Tis warm."

"And you're a liar," Æsa said, crossing her arms. A deep laugh erupted from Gustaf as he spun to face her. The sound of his joy warmed her very soul, and she smiled. "I believe that's the first time I've ever heard you laugh, my lord."

He held her gaze for a moment as if pondering this revelation. "With you by my side as my wife, I trust 'twill not be the last. You bring much happiness to me."

Gustaf's words caressed her as soothingly as if his own hand had stroked her body. She basked in this moment, for in all her years of captivity, she'd never known the blessing of peace, much less a man who wanted to live out the rest of his days with her at his side.

She'd felt the curses and mockery of the gods for so long, she'd almost begun to give up hope of ever finding joy and love. Had the gods finally taken pity on her? Was Gustaf a gift from Odin for all the days she'd spent suffering and praying for a reprieve?

To her, Gustaf was more than a gift. He was the promise of a better life. Her every desire. Her single greatest reason to live.

Gustaf splashed the water around him before dunking under, disappearing beneath its surface. As quickly as he sank into its shallow depths, he emerged a drenched man who resembled a demigod. His long golden hair clung to his neck and shoulders, and the clear mountain water fell off his body as if it worshipped every inch of male muscle on the way down.

"Are you not going to join me?" he asked, opening his arms invitingly.

Knowing how cold the water was, she shook her head. "I shall take more pleasure in watching you."

"Suit yourself." He drew in a large breath and sank like a stone. The constant lateral movement of the stream made it difficult to see where he'd gone. She stepped away from the edge, suspicious that he'd reemerge and haul her in by surprise. Finally, he came up at the far side of the stream, the current rushing past him in foamy bubbles. He plucked a single flower from the hillside at the water's edge, and the muscles in his back flexed as he brought the purple blossom to his nose. His eyes closed as he drew in a deep breath.

Æsa watched him examine the delicate bud. He brushed his finger over its colored petal before smelling it again. Her hulking Northman appeared capable of crushing a man's skull with his large, powerful hands, yet a fragile blossom had nothing to fear in his keeping.

In his arms, Æsa felt the same. Though he might have possessed the strength of three men, his touch upon her skin was whisper soft. For a moment, she felt jealous of the flower gently pinched between his fingers that was stealing all his attention. As the warm light of the afternoon sun bounced off his shoulders and glistened over his damp, bronze skin, she was unable to resist him anymore. She ignored the cool temperature water separating them and unfastened the cloak from her shoulders.

Gustaf glanced up, and a half smile twitched his lips. He pinned her with a look that nearly stopped her heart, and, with the flower still in his hand, he closed the distance between them. Each step was as purposeful as the last until the stream rescinded enough to expose his lower half one small, blessed degree at a time.

Chapter Six

Gustaf stopped directly in front of her and presented the flower. "For you, my dearest Æsa." He tucked the bloom behind her ear and brushed her hair off her shoulder. "You're so beautiful."

Æsa blushed to a lovely pale pink, and he knew from experience that the flush of her skin extended beyond her face and neck. Eager to catch a glimpse of the rosy tint flushing her breasts, he gripped the fabric of her tunic in his fists and raised it over her head. Before he could stop himself, he pulled her into his embrace and relished the warmth of her naked skin soothing the harsh cold from his body.

But only for a moment.

He then swept her up in his arms and carried her into the stream

"Nay, my lord! Please!" Æsa screamed, clutching his neck. She bucked and wriggled to escape his hold, but he ignored her desperate pleas and tossed her into the water.

Immediately, she sprang forward and climbed his body like a tree to escape the cold. He held her tightly in his arms, enjoying the feel of their wet, naked bodies clinging to each other for warmth. Gustaf should have felt guilty for throwing her in, but her reaction kept him from feeling any remorse, especially when she cursed him with a venomous tongue.

"You ad-d-dle brained s-s-sod!" she stammered, convulsively shivering. "I sh-sh-should c-c-castrate you f-f-or this!"

Undeterred by the sadistic threats she made on his precious genitalia, he ravaged the mouth that spat such vicious words. At first, she fought to be kissed, pounding on his chest in retaliation. He had no idea how arousing it was to steal a kiss from her, but he knew she wouldn't be unwilling for long.

Eventually, her fists unclenched and wound around his neck, threading in his hair. Tugging. Clawing to get closer. The scrape of her nails on his scalp sent shivers throughout his body as he hauled her out of the water and staggered along the well-worn path back to the small stone cottage. He burst through the door and welcomed the warmth enveloping them in a blanket of dry heat and soft amber light.

Tangled together, they made their way to the single boxbed along the wall. Æsa refused to let go, and he refused to stop kissing her. His Æsa.

My wife.

The echo of that word in his brain sounded better than anything in the world. He'd spent so much of his life without the love and affection of a woman that he long feared it was the will of the gods. He'd deemed it was his calling to die honorably on a battlefield or in the throes of dutiful vengeance, and he'd readily embrace whatever path Odin laid out for him.

But now, his course had taken a sharp turn. With his father avenged and Æsa in his arms, his days of living and dying by the sword were over. He could finally hang up his weapon and raise a family as he'd always dreamed.

He laid her down upon the furs that covered the crude straw bedding of the boxbed and planted a soft kiss on the inside of her right wrist. He drew in the familiar scent of lavender and primrose, then stepped backward to throw some more turf logs on the fire that had barely begun to burn.

Out of the smoke, hungry flames lapped the turf, and soon the room glowed. Muted orange and red hues cast over every object surrounding the hearth, including his lovely maiden. The smooth skin of her calf shimmered in the firelight as she bent her knee. He swallowed hard as his gaze followed the path of her hand from the outside of her shapely thigh, over the curve of her hip, and up to the swell of her breast.

He came to her, his gaze locked on the taut pink nipple he craved to take into his mouth. It was all he could do not to ravish her. He'd spent the better part of his journey from Inishmore to Skúvoy fantasizing about all the things he wanted to do to Æsa upon his return, none of which were hurried or brief. In fact, he wanted to take his time with her. Savor her. Kiss every inch of her ivory skin. Nibble every freckle dotted across her shoulders. And make slow, agonizing love to her until neither of them had the strength to move.

He lowered himself upon her and captured her lips in a deep, ravenous kiss. The scent of lavender, primrose, and peat filled the air as he cradled her body against him and pushed inside her. Like two wild flames, they fused as one, body and soul.

Chapter Seven

A fit of muffled male laughter broke the pleasantry of Gustaf's dreams. He moaned and stirred about in his bed, and reached across the boxbed for Æsa. He sought her warm body with a sluggish hand, patting the spot where she had once lain entangled with him. When he found the place beside him empty and cool to the touch, his eyes shot open. The blurry sight of seven men sitting around his hearth came into view, and he sat up with a jolt.

"Sleep well, m'lord?" Jørgen asked coolly.

"Where's Æsa?"

"Out back. Perhaps gathering the pile of clothing you two left behind along the stream."

He glanced down at himself and the warm hide that hardly covered his lower half. "Is she...?"

"Walking about as naked as her lover?" Jørgen finished for him. "Nay."

A brief spell of snickering hissed around the fire, but Gustaf didn't say anything to stop it. He'd only look like a fool barking orders in the nude.

"How long have I been asleep?" he finally inquired, running a hand down his tired face.

"Long enough for us to hear you talk in your slumber," Snorri remarked.

Gustaf paused midstroke, glancing between each man. "I don't talk in my sleep."

"Tell that to my ears. I had to listen to you long into the evening."

Gustaf sat helpless as Snorri lay his head on Jørgen's shoulder and imitated him in his sleep, spouting off exaggerated words of affection about Æsa. A few more joined in, offering their best impersonation of their chieftain in love, each one more inflated than the next.

"Enough," Gustaf barked. "If you didn't want to hear it, you could've left and found your own lodging."

"And miss the soft, delicate side of the eldest warrior son of Rælik?" Snorri badgered. "I think not."

Gustaf rolled his eyes and slouched back into the boxbed. It was useless trying to convince Snorri of anything. He was either ridiculing or complaining whenever he opened his mouth.

As Gustaf was about to roll out of bed, a shrill, high-pitched shriek erupted seconds before a bird dove in flight from the rafters and landed on Øyven's forearm. Gustaf glowered at Øyven sitting at the far corner of the room. "Odin's blood, what is that?"

Øyven glanced at the bird. "'Tis a falcon, m'lord."

Gustaf was not amused. "I know what it is. Why is it in here?"

"I traded for her at the harbor," Øyven said

admiringly, watching the bird snatch a morsel of food from his gloved hand. "Is she not beautiful?"

Gustaf grunted.

"She is smart too," Øyven added. "She already knows to come to me."

"It doesn't take much intelligence for a starving bird to come where food is offered," Snorri sneered.

Øyven didn't so much as bat an eye at the insult. Instead, he continued to smile and appreciate the bird as it perched on his wrist.

"Have you a cage for it?" Gustaf asked.

Øyven's mood instantly dropped. "Aye."

By the look on Øyven's face, Gustaf knew he didn't want to trap the bird behind bars unless absolutely necessary. The lad's sensitivity to animals reminded him of himself as a boy learning to hunt. It had taken a long time for Gustaf to become accustomed to trapping and killing game. In fact, he recalled his mother once saying that because of his respect for living things, he'd be the best hunter there was because he'd be sure to make each kill swift and humane. Those skills also made him a deadly warrior against his enemies. Many would attest to it, if they could speak beyond the grave.

"If I must cage her, m'lord," Øyven said reluctantly, "I will."

Gustaf suddenly had a change of heart. "The bird can remain free for now. Just make certain she's caged when we're at sea. I would hate for it to fly away in the transport before you've had a chance to train it properly."

Øyven's smile returned. "Thank you."

"That chicken better not shit on me while I'm sleeping tonight," Snorri warned. "Or else I might have to boil off her feathers and eat her for breakfast."

"For that little remark, I hope she does," muttered Øyven. "'Twill not only prove her to be intelligent but also a good judge of character."

Snorri didn't look impressed. "Clever birds taste just as good as dimwitted ones."

Gustaf laughed. "You'd do best to keep that falcon of yours out of Snorri's reach, Øyven. We all know how much the man likes to eat. Speaking of which, I assume you wretches set aside some fish for me?"

Jørgen handed Gustaf a wooden bowl full of charred herring. "I think you'll find your woman to be a skilled cook."

His mouth watered as he lifted the savory fish to his nose. Before he took his first bite, he gave Jørgen a look of severity. "Please tell me Æsa ate three fish, as I instructed."

"Of course, m'lord."

Pleased with his friend's answer, he bit into the tender meat and closed his eyes as he savored it. An abundance of flavor from herbs he'd never tasted before filled his mouth. He devoured the first fish, then started on the second, humming with satisfaction. "Æsa made this?"

"Indeed, I did." Æsa entered the room carrying an armful of clothing and a bucket of fresh water. "Do you like it?"

He answered with an overzealous nod and bolted the rest to feed his growling stomach.

"That makes me very happy, m'lord," she said, blushing.

Æsa made him very happy. Licking each finger, he watched as she placed his boots on the floor and folded his clothes in a neat pile on the table. After that, she bustled around the room, refilling each man's cup. She was a natural, he noted, and seemed at ease with his men's company, offering casual conversation as she went. He admired the way she took charge and tended to their needs. Even Snorri seemed pleased. The number of times Gustaf saw the man grin when she filled his cup indicated he was less cantankerous than usual.

He also noticed the kirtle she wore was a different one from this morning. She was now dressed in the tunic he'd purchased for her before he left the isle a month ago. The shade of blue went well with the light hue of her eyes, and the scarlet embroidery coordinated with the vibrant color of her hair. The fabric hugged her curves in all the right places, despite the slight weight she'd lost. He concluded she must have altered it recently, proving her adept with a needle and thread as well.

What struck him most, however, was seeing her move about with a casual grace akin to a noble woman's charm and elegance. Where she'd learned that was a mystery to him as her past hadn't allowed for such proper culturing.

She must have come by it naturally.

His mother would be proud.

Gustaf then smiled at the thought of seeing Æsa as a wife and mother; sewing clothes, cooking dinner at the hearth, and tending to all sorts of domestic duties as his equal head of household. He imagined a flock of giggling children tugging at her skirt as she busied herself about their home. He'd build a spacious longhouse, of course, to accommodate all the children he wanted to have with her.

As he continued to admire her, they eventually locked eyes, and an unspoken appreciation registered between them. Æsa's gaze fell over his bare chest, and she smiled as if calling to mind the long, passionate moments she'd spent tangled up with him, making sweet love before they'd fallen asleep in each other's arms. He too thought about how perfect their reuniting had been after being away from each other for so long, until she turned abruptly, fanned her face, and set to filling a wooden cup for him.

Immediately, he stood and drew the hide around his waist. With it secured in his fist, he walked toward her, ignoring the group of men sitting on the floor around the hearth. "You look lovely."

She smiled and handed him the cup. "As do you. 'Tis a pity you must get dressed."

He accepted the drink and held it up in a toast-like fashion. "'Tis a pity my men figured out how to fish."

Snorri cleared his throat behind them. "We would've returned sooner had it not been for Øyven bartering for the bird. Go on. Tell him what you traded for it, Øyven."

Gustaf tipped the cup to his lips and turned toward his men. The look on Øyven's face spoke volumes over the significance of the price. "What *did* you offer in exchange for the falcon?"

Øyven glanced between Gustaf and Snorri, reluctant to say. Out of patience, Snorri spoke for him. "He gave away his sword—the one thing a warrior needs to survive in this godforsaken world. He might as well have cut off his cock."

Øyven's jaw clenched. "With all due respect, m'lord, I've brandished my sword for your father and for my own. 'Twas a worthy cause, and I'd do it again. But now, I'm through fighting. I have no need for my sword any longer. I want to live in peace." He threw Snorri a look of defiance. "What is wrong with that?"

"'Tis foolhardy and senseless, boy. Witty words are never enough where peace is concerned." Snorri eyed Gustaf carefully, holding his gaze. "We all know how that sad story ended."

Gustaf narrowed his eyes. "Are you saying my father died in vain?"

Snorri scoffed. "Harald Fairhair—the man who issued your father's death warrant so many years ago—has seized the land you once called home, gained more popularity than the late Alfred, King of Wessex, and continues to sit high on his noble throne. He feasts on the fruits from the very soil fertilized with your father's blood. You tell me, m'lord, if his death was in vain."

An awkward silence fell upon the group. Snorri had made his point well by invoking the one thing about which Gustaf was very passionate. Harald Fairhair might not have held the dagger that killed his father, but his hands were just as bloody as the ten he'd paid to do the deed. Gustaf had dedicated so many years of his life to finding those who were directly responsible for his father's murder that taking on the king who funded it seemed insignificant at the time. Now that Snorri had laid it out before him in such an irrefutable and straightforward fashion, he had no idea what to say in reply.

In all honesty, Gustaf had no desire to go after the King of Norway. The man was more powerful than any army Gustaf could assemble. He had more wealth than all the nobles of Wessex and Mercia combined, and he wielded more authority than the Christian pope of Rome. As far as Gustaf was concerned, Fairhair was untouchable.

A tender caress on Gustaf's forearm broke his reverie.

"If I may…?" Æsa asked.

Her fingertips calmed his pounding heart and soothed his weary mind. He had no worldly idea what guidance Æsa could offer on this complex issue, but he was certainly willing to hear it. He gestured with a deep nod of his head. "By all means."

Æsa scanned the seven faces now staring at her intently, and rocked on her heels in nervousness. "Like myself, many of you have lost family to Harald's cruel reign. We all know what he's capable of and how far he's willing to go to secure a vast domain across Scandinavia. But may I remind you that your loved ones died so you might live." Æsa glanced at Gustaf and meekly smiled. "Someone once told me there is no greater love than when a man lays down his life for another." She squared her shoulders and affixed her gaze back upon his men. "Love is never in vain. I've seen many reasons why men draw their swords. Some for riches. Some for notoriety. Some over women, and some over the last drop of mead. All are without honor, except for love." She hung her head in sadness. "Or for freedom... So, nay, I say to you, Snorri. Gustaf's father died not in vain. 'Twas for love that he gave his life."

Chapter Eight

Gustaf closed the door behind him as he and Æsa stepped into the brisk evening air. The golden sun set low on the horizon, highlighting her cinnamon locks with streaks of glistening honey. Bejeweled and dressed in noble attire, she'd commanded the entire room with her poignant oration about love and sacrifice. To him, she'd never looked more beautiful.

"Why do you look at me like that?" Æsa asked.

"I'm proud of you" he replied, "and the stance you made on my father's behalf." He heard a tiny sound come from her chest, much like a scoff as she turned away. He reached for her and spun her around to face him. "I mean what I say." He gave her arms a gentle squeeze. "No one has ever been able to shut Snorri's mouth as fast as you did. I believe you rendered him speechless."

She hid a smile behind pursed lips. "I suppose I did. But I shouldn't have interfered."

He tipped her chin upward. "Why?"

"Because 'twas not my place."

"Your place is beside me."

"As your attentive, obedient wife," she added. "Not as

an outspoken whor—"

"Careful," Gustaf warned. He watched as her rounded lips altered the sound of her initial word.

"…woman…who meddles in her lord's affairs."

Gustaf grinned his approval. "I commend you on your supplementary word choice, my dearest Æsa, but I cannot agree with your reasoning. You didn't meddle in my affairs. You assisted me when I was at a loss." He took her hand and cupped it between his, kissing the top of her wrist. "You said what I could not."

She looked at him skeptically. "My words mirrored *your* thoughts? Surely you jest."

With a flick of his hand, he tugged her into his arms. Her sudden gasp and sweet scent inflamed his senses, and he breathed her in. "Why is that so hard to believe? You and I having similar thoughts."

"Because we are so different."

Gustaf looked deep into her eyes. "What makes you think we are different?"

"Well, there is the obvious."

To his surprise, Æsa cupped him between the legs with about as much strength as one would grasp a sword hilt. He flinched at first, then chuckled. "Aye, there is that. What else?"

She pondered. "You're a respected warrior and leader. When you talk, men listen. When you unsheathe your sword, men quake in their boots."

"And when you draw a bow, men drop to their knees."

"Hardly, m'lord."

"Dispute it all you want, but as I recall, this respected warrior and leader had to make good use of his shield to protect himself. For a moment there, I thought it was the end. Arrows whizzed past my head, inches from my skull. I prayed to Odin and offered myself to Thor that if I must die right here on the hillock of Skúvoy at the feet of Æsa 'the Wild,' 'twould be an honorable death."

She giggled at his exaggerated tale, eyes twinkling. "Is that your way of praising me so that I might become an archer or shield-maiden?"

Gustaf nipped at her lips. "You enjoyed it too much not to."

"Is that so?"

"I think it is." He ruminated over her possible emotions at the time of using the bow. "At first, I think you felt empowered, knowing you were singlehandedly holding off a group of dangerous men—albeit their leader was roguishly handsome."

Æsa wrapped her arms more tightly around his back. "Go on."

"I wager you even had thoughts of taking their leader prisoner and using his manly body for your own personal pleasure."

"Hmm…perhaps."

Her devious grin spurred an assortment of lustful thoughts in his head. "You continued to cast off a barrage of arrows, your thighs quivering at the thought of straddling said leader. Then realization sank in. You felt an immense pang of sorrow and regret knowing you could have killed him."

"Are we still talking about the roguishly handsome leader or you?"

Gustaf whipped her body around and pinned her against the outside wall of the cottage. "See? We are not so different. We share the same thoughts, and we *want* the same things. And right now, I want you."

A subtle clearing of a throat interrupted their private moment. Gustaf snapped his head to the right and squinted into the shadowy darkness of dusk. "Jørgen?"

"Aye, m'lord."

Æsa slipped from Gustaf's embrace, smoothed her tunic, and tucked a loose strand of hair behind her ear. He pulled her back into his arms and playfully popped a loud kiss on her lips. "This had better be important, Jørgen."

"I wouldn't dare disturb you if 'twere not."

"Very well," Gustaf said. He kissed Æsa once more, this time with purpose and tenderness. "Would you excuse us?"

"As you wish, m'lord."

Gustaf watched her leave, a glint of sadness overcoming him with her departure. He crossed his arms and leaned his shoulder against the stone face of the cottage. "I'm listening."

Jørgen stepped forward and handed Gustaf his sword and scabbard. "I believe we're being watched, m'lord."

Chapter Nine

Gustaf took a much-needed breath and blew it out in exasperation, gazing at the scabbard that sheathed his weapon. He'd finally begun to enjoy himself as a man who'd hung up the proverbial sword. A warrior who'd treasure the last days of his adult life as a common man whose only aim was to provide for his future wife and family.

Living in secret and fighting with stealth were supposed to be a thing of the past. Perhaps Jørgen was only being paranoid.

"Are we being watched at this moment?" Gustaf asked.

Jørgen glanced nonchalantly over his shoulder behind him. "I believe so, m'lord. I sent Snorri to scout the area and to take first watch."

Gustaf looked at him skeptically. "And who, may I ask, is observing us?"

"I can't say for certain," Jørgen admitted, his voice growing quieter. "I first sensed it when we were fishing. Whenever I looked around, the same four men were always eyeing us."

"Should I remind you we are on the Faroes? Half the people who inhabit this isle look suspicious of something. And most are rogues and fugitives, running to escape Harald Fairhair."

"I'm well aware of the unfavorable company this island keeps. But I assure you, 'tis more than just a silly suspicion. They seemed to be measuring us, sizing up our numbers before they plot a strike against us."

"And for what?" Gustaf asked, cocking his head. "I've nothing of value here, except Æsa." As soon as he said it, his heart dropped to his stomach. She mattered more to him than any gold or silver on earth. "If they're after her, they'll be making a grave mistake. I'll die before I let anyone have her."

"Which is why I said not a word in front of her. I didn't want her to worry needlessly."

Incited by the thought of someone plotting to take Æsa from him, he fastened his sword and scabbard around his waist. Though he still had his doubts why someone else would value her enough to risk life against Gustaf and his seven skilled warriors, he'd at least be prepared for the worst. "'Twas wise of you to keep silence where Æsa is concerned. Are the others aware?"

"Aye, m'lord."

Gustaf clasped his friend's shoulder. "Keep watch with Snorri. I'll pay a visit to Didrik, the eyes and ears of this isle. He might know something about these men."

"And where do I tell Æsa you've gone?"

He thought for a moment. "Tell her I went to see Didrik to settle my debt with him and say my farewells. I'll not be long."

****

Gustaf stood at the door of Didrik's home and watched smoke rise from the outlet hole of the roof. He hated to bother the man at such an hour, but Æsa's safety was his biggest priority. Surely he'd understand.

Gustaf raised his hand to knock, but the door flew open and revealed Didrik with a drawn bow and arrow taking aim. The gray-bearded old man's eyes grew wide with surprise.

"Gustaf!" Didrik cheered, lowering his weapon. "Come in. Come in. Forgive me."

Gustaf breathed a little easier as he entered and closed the door behind him. The aroma of spices—the same ones Æsa used on the fish she'd cooked him—turf, smoke, and dried skerpikjøt filled the room. Between the herbs hanging from the rafters and the weapon Didrik wielded, it seemed that his old friend had spent more time with Æsa than he realized.

"So, 'twas you who taught my Æsa the bow."

Didrik chuckled and sat on a bench by the fire, gesturing for Gustaf to join him. "She was quick to learn. I saw she was efficient enough to give you and your men pause."

Gustaf sat beside him. "You saw that, did you?"

Didrik handed him a weathered, wooden cup filled with mead. "I see everything on this isle."

Gustaf gladly accepted the drink, thankful to have something stronger than the water. He drank until it was gone and handed it back. "That's exactly my reason for visiting you at this hour, my old friend. Jørgen seems to think we're being watched by a few crooked men. Four stragglers down by the harbor."

"Five to be exact," Didrik corrected. "The other one stays out of sight most of the time while the four do his bidding. They sailed in a few days before you did and have kept to themselves for the most part. Like eels, they loiter inconspicuously, but they can't hide the hunger in their eyes."

Gustaf didn't need to ask for whom they hungered. By the look Didrik shot him, he knew it was Æsa. Every hair on the back of his neck stood up, and his stomach soured. "Why her?"

The old man scoffed. "Isn't it obvious?"

Aye, Æsa was a tempting, rare find. Her red hair was like silk, long and radiant down her back. Her breasts were firm, round, and voluptuous. And her luscious, full lips could bring just about any man to his knees. But her beauty didn't make him any more willing to share with others.

"If they truly wanted her," Gustaf asked, "why did they not strike when they had the chance? When there was no one to guard her?"

"My guess is they wanted to, but they've since realized they lost their opportunity now that you've returned," Didrik said.

"Then why do they continue to watch my men?"

"Men are covetous beings, Gustaf. You of all men know that after what happened to your father. And it takes a longer spell for the gluttonous ones to move on to something else less worthwhile. That being said," Didrik added, pouring another cup of mead from the ewer at his feet, "I wouldn't hang around long enough to test their determination."

Didrik handed Gustaf a filled cup, and Gustaf drank heavily, letting the cool, honeyed liquid soothe his hot, dry throat. No one had yet to challenge him over Æsa, but it was the notion of a few wayward men giving it thought that burned his arse.

"Rest assured, we shall leave the isle before sunrise." He retrieved a small pouch from his person and offered it to Didrik. "This is for all your help."

The old man pushed it away. "My knowledge is free. It spills from my mouth, even to those who are deaf and penniless."

Gustaf stood and tossed it into his lap anyway.

Didrik picked it up and tested its weight in his hand. "Friendship is free as well, you know."

"Aye, but friendship doesn't keep you warm through the winter, nor does it fill your gut with food. Consider it a gift for all that you have done for me. For Æsa."

"'Twas an honor to watch over the girl while you were gone," he said, standing as well. "Am I to assume you'll not be coming back?"

Gustaf didn't like good-byes any more than the next man, but once he saw to his men's safe return home, he'd set sail for his family on Inishmore and never look back. He embraced Didrik, patting him soundly. "May Odin keep his watchful eye over you, and may I see you in Valhalla one fine day."

"'Twill take more than one god's eye to shelter this old goat. I'll see you in Valhalla, this you can be sure, for I'll be damned if I die a straw death."

Gustaf laughed and turned to leave. "Until then…farewell, my friend."

Stepping out into the pitch of night, he gazed into the darkness and waited. He drew his sword, half expecting to be assaulted by the men he'd just inquired about. To his relief, he stood unharmed. Perhaps ignored. Or maybe he was out of his damn mind.

Scolding himself for letting his paranoia run away with his good sense, he sheathed his weapon and journeyed up the hill to the one place he felt sane: Æsa's arms.

****

Æsa opened her eyes and saw Gustaf tiptoeing between the bodies of his snoring men lying scattered about the rush-covered floor around the hearth. She watched him add a few more turf logs to the fire, eager for when he'd join her in the warmth of her bed.

He looked powerful and haughty as he stood in the golden glow of the flames. The shadow of his dark beard framed an equally strong jaw. She noticed the sword at his hip and wondered if he chose to wear it out of necessity or habit. He'd proclaimed his days of wielding such a weapon were over, but his eyes, dark and brooding, said differently.

"What troubles you, m'lord?" she whispered.

He looked up at her, startled. "I thought you were asleep. Did I wake you?"

"Nay. I was waiting for you. Come to bed."

Gustaf quietly padded toward her and unbuckled his belt in the process. After removing his weapon, he kicked off his boots and slipped beneath the hides, pulling her close. She relished the feel of the pure strength in his arms and the natural male warmth he brought as he snuggled around her.

"Are you going to tell me what troubles you, or must I ask Jørgen and Snorri, who are outside taking first watch?"

"How do you know they aren't taking a piss?"

"That is quite a long piss, m'lord."

Gustaf's deep chuckle rumbled against her back. "So 'tis," he said, heaving a heavy leg over hers and kissing her shoulder. "Fret not, my dearest Æsa. 'Tis only to safeguard you."

"From whom?"

"No one in particular. Now, close your eyes."

"Why must two men lose their sleep over me?"

"Because I deem it so."

She twisted in his arms and caught his gaze. "Do your men always do as you say?"

"Without fail. Unlike someone I know who cannot follow a simple command." He poked her forehead and flashed a stern look as if trying to impose his authority over her.

She glanced at the straight line of his lips and touched her fingertip to them, lightly tracing the contour of his mouth. "You still haven't told me what troubles you."

Gustaf reached out and toyed with a strand of her hair. "Nothing troubles me save for the fact that your eyes are, in spite of my insistence, open. Need I remind you of the long journey we have ahead of us?" He spun her back around and caged her within his arms as he spooned against her.

She felt the heat of his supple lips and the rasp of his prickly beard as he kissed her shoulder, her neck, and her ear. The sensation of the trail he blazed on her skin lingered while she lay in the confines of his heavy limbs.

"Close your eyes, Æsa, and worry no more over me. I'm here, and I'm yours."

A long, contented sigh was her only response. He smiled and stroked her hair, sinking into the straw and fleece cushioning the boxbed. He listened to the sound of her deep, even breaths and the crackle of the warm fire at his back. This was where he'd dreamed of being for so long, and he savored this rare, peaceful moment.

Holding Æsa, pleasing her, protecting her; those were now his only missions in life.

Chapter Ten

Asmundr observed the small cottage nestled in the hilltop and the two men who stood guard. He absently groped himself as he thought of the redhead inside. He'd known her well throughout the years, well enough to remember the weight of her breasts and the curve of her bottom as he forcefully took her one fateful evening...

His father, Ragnar, had brought the girl home from the slave market several years ago and abused her about as much as he exercised his right to mate with her when his other wives wouldn't. Asmundr couldn't stand the sight of his own father and had spent many nights plotting Ragnar's death and saving the servant girl from further degradation.

One night, while his father convened with his trusted men, Asmundr sneaked into Æsa's chamber. He'd planned to make her understand the depths of his feelings and then kill his father to prove it. To his surprise, he caught Æsa with her ear to the door, listening in on his father's private conversation on the other side.

Knowing the discussion was over some ridiculous amount of silver Harald Fairhair paid his father to kill some wealthy chieftain who would not bow down, and its whereabouts, Asmundr proposed that they could run away and find the buried stash together. The girl panicked and denied hearing anything.

She wounded him greatly. He'd confided in her and confessed his evil plan against his own father, and she still didn't trust him. He tried to sympathize with Æsa's fear, for he too had been prisoner to cowardice all his life, and had come to realize that words of promise and sacrifice were not enough. She needed to be shown.

He chased her around the room and eventually pinned her on the boxbed. She squirmed beneath him, and he grew hard with the feel of her sex rubbing his. If he were aroused, surely she was too.

Asmundr lifted her skirts, but she smacked him across the face. "Do not be like your father," she warned. "He is a vile man, and you'll be no different if you do this."

Her last words had cut him so deep that what he'd done next wasn't his fault. She'd pushed him too far.

He rolled her over and showed her as little mercy as his despicable father. Deep down, he knew she enjoyed it. She was a whore. She didn't know any other way. And he enjoyed his father bursting into the room and witnessing it. The shock and rage in his father's eyes was worth all the silver in the world, and it came as no surprise that Asmundr was banished from Iceland.

What he hadn't expected was finding out that his father had spared Æsa's life and sent another to end his.

Fortunately for Asmundr, it had taken only a handful of coins to pay the mercenary off and return with news that Ragnar's son was dead.

Asmundr returned to Iceland a few years later to kill his father once and for all, but someone had already beaten him to it. He found Ragnar drawn and hanged from the rafter of his longhouse by his own intestines. It seemed as though his father's cruel, dark past had finally caught up with him, and no amount of silver was enough to save him.

Asmundr crouched behind a large boulder in the dark, assessing the number of warriors who guarded one worthless *thrall* as if she were a princess of Norway. He was convinced of two things—these were the men who'd killed his father, and the redhead was the manipulative bitch who knew where his father's silver was buried.

"How will you get to her now, m'lord?" Grimr asked.

"All in good time, Grimr," he stated coolly.

"Do you think she is after Ragnar's buried silver?"

Asmundr controlled his temper and lowered his voice, mindful of the two guards within earshot. "You mean *my* silver," he corrected. "I think she's biding her time with these imbeciles and wooing the big one long enough to get him to do whatever she desires. If 'tis my silver she seeks, we shall be one step ahead of her."

****

The sharp screech of a falcon and the beat of its wings brought Æsa to a waking jolt. She sat up and found that the space beside her where Gustaf had slept was empty. She also noticed that the men, who once lay strewn about the floor, were gone as were the contents of the room. What little they possessed had been packed up and most likely loaded upon Gustaf's ship for departure. When he said they'd leave at the first light of dawn, he meant it.

Øyven came through the door with a bucket half-full of water and saw that Æsa had awakened. He nodded in greeting but didn't have a word to say. Instead, he doused the fire in the hearth and picked up his bird's cage.

"Have you seen Gustaf?" she asked before he could carry it outside.

"He took watch all night after you fell asleep, m'lady. I'll tell him you're awake."

Æsa thanked Øyven and waited for him to walk out the door before she flung her feet over the side of the bed. The acrid smell of soot and wet peat drifted in a thick band of gray smoke up her nose as she stood and stretched.

"I trust you slept well."

The familiar voice of her future husband startled her from her reverie, and she turned to find him standing at the doorway. Honestly, she couldn't remember a time when she'd slept so soundly. Having Gustaf around was not only promising where her happiness was concerned, but he proved to have an effect on her sleep as well.

She smiled upon his approach and threw her arms

around his neck. "I slept extremely well because I thought you were by my side. But I hear you took watch through the night."

Gustaf swept her up in his embrace, and his heady male scent pervaded her senses. He bent to kiss her, his lips warm and soft. "If I recall, someone was upset that two men were losing sleep over her. So, I lessened the number to one."

Æsa shook her head. "Since when have you ever obeyed anything I've said?"

"Since I'm soon to be married to you. I'm practicing being the dutiful husband."

She drew her finger around his chest in thought. "If you want to be dutiful, then perhaps you should think about a husband's duty to his wife in bed. She has needs too, you know, and they can't be met when her husband is outside gazing at stars."

His hearty laughter vibrated through her entire being. "Is that what you think I was doing?"

"I know you weren't in here making love to me."

Gustaf gathered her hands in his and brought them to his lips, kissing the top of each. "Now that I know, I shall promise to be more devoted to my betrothed in bed."

"And obey her every word?" Æsa added.

He laughed and swatted her behind. "Don't push it." Øyven's falcon squawked in the distance, and Gustaf was redirected. "Have you tended to your morning ablutions, then?"

"I have not," she said

"Come. I shall guard you as you do." He tugged her along by the hand and out the back door.

"Is it really necessary that you accompany me?"

She heard him sigh. "It makes me feel better to know you're safe. Now, be quick about it."

"Or else?" she baited, adding an extra shimmy to her hips as she sauntered toward the stream.

Gustaf watched the alluring sway of her bottom as she disappeared behind a bush along the water's edge. And what a lovely backside it was. He drew in a deep breath and tried to tamp down his own needs and desires that she so effortlessly stirred in him. She'd barely bat an eye, and he'd fall under her spell. He was a weak man for it and couldn't afford to be distracted right now. With Æsa in possible danger, he needed to be more alert than ever.

"My lord," Jørgen announced as he approached at a safe distance. "The men are on the *langskip* and await your command. No sign of the others." He handed Gustaf a long woolen cloak.

"What is this?" Gustaf asked.

"Didrik said Æsa might need it for the journey. 'Twas his wife's."

Gustaf inspected the garment, and the large, cavernous hood caught his eye. It would be perfect for hiding Æsa's fiery hair. If the vagrants were keeping a close watch on a redheaded female, then perhaps he could slip her past their attention if the one thing they'd be looking for was hidden.

The fact that they held such a keen interest in Æsa ate at his heart. What if Jørgen hadn't convinced him to turn the longship around and bring her along? What kind of trouble would she have been in? His stomach dropped at the thought.

"Is everything all right?" Jørgen asked as though sensing his discontentment.

Gustaf dismissed his concerns, as they were nothing worth fretting over. He was there, and Æsa was safe. No harm had been done. "Everything is fine. In fact," he admitted optimistically, "nothing could be better. I've asked Æsa to be my wife, and she accepted. Isn't that right, love?"

"'Tis a good match, m'lord," Jørgen replied.

"Æsa?" Gustaf called. "Æsa, are you all right?" When she didn't respond, the cold hand of dread wrapped around his throat. He bolted toward the stream with Jørgen on his heels, and when they rounded the shrubbery, they found Æsa staring into the water.

"Æsa," Gustaf said in exasperation, pulling her to her feet by her elbow. "Why did you not answer me?" Her face was white and her eyes wide with fear, staring into nothingness. While his heartbeat settled, he took great pains to quiet his voice. "What happened? What has frightened you?" He shook her hard when she did not answer. "Æsa, speak!"

Finally, her frozen stare fell on him. "Are you certain

you killed Ragnar?"

Her question took Gustaf by complete surprise. He looked to Jørgen first, seeing that his befuddlement matched his own, and back toward Æsa. He squeezed her arms in a soothing manner before he testified to the harrowing truth. "Ragnar is dead." Images of the man gutted and dangling from his insides flashed in his mind. He cringed at the memory of the man's scream but immediately blocked out the sound as soon as it echoed in his ears. He swallowed hard, keeping the gruesome details to himself. "No man could've survived. He is dead. I assure you."

She extended a shaky finger toward the water's edge, her bottom lip quivering as she spoke. "Then why is his ring here? There…'tis his."

Gustaf squinted along the bank, and a glint of something shiny caught his attention. Tucked amid the soft mud and rocks was a silver ring. He squatted and picked it up, swishing it in the water until it was clean. There was pagan motif of intertwining beasts encrusted over one large ruby. Though he wished he hadn't remembered, he recalled this very ring on Ragnar's finger as he hung stock-still in death. If that were so, how did it travel from Ragnar's hand to the Faroes? And how was it possible that Æsa should find it?

Unless it was planted with that exact purpose in mind.

Gustaf hid Æsa behind his back and searched the surrounding landscape. He unsheathed his sword and

Jørgen did the same.

"If Ragnar is dead, how did his ring wind up here?" Æsa asked, her voice strained. "Did you take it from him?"

Gustaf spun to face her, abhorring her accusation. "I took naught from him but his life."

"Then how—"

"I know not," Gustaf interrupted harshly. He pitched the ring over the hillside and threw Didrik's cloak over Æsa's head, making sure every strand of hair was tucked inside. He then took her by the hand and tugged her down the hill to his longship. He would not play games with these vagrants. Whoever toyed with him and tormented Æsa would surely pay.

****

Asmundr came out of his hiding place and stooped to pick up his father's ring, sliding it back on his right hand. He twisted it around his finger and smiled with unremorseful gratification.

"You're a cruel man, m'lord," Grimr praised.

"I've only just begun, my friend."

"What do we do now?" Grimr asked.

Asmundr gave him a sideways glance. "Why, we follow them, of course."

Chapter Eleven

Gustaf gripped the steer board of his ship short of breaking it off with his fist. Having Æsa safely aboard his longship gave him only a temporary sense of relief, as it did little to ease his temper. Whoever was playing mind games with him had made it personal. They'd targeted the one precious thing in his life, and if they thought they could get to her without a fight, they were sorely mistaken.

Focused onward, he navigated his ship east toward Skíringssalr while his men rowed with as much determination in their backs and arms as he had in his racing heart. If he could get to familiar land, he'd gain the upper hand and have a better chance of keeping Æsa safe. Right now, he felt like a pawn, his every move calculated by his foes before he made it. He wasn't used to being the prey, and before this was over, he'd make whoever was responsible wish they hadn't meddled with the eldest son of Rælik.

Once they were farther out to sea, Gustaf gave the order to erect the mast and rig the sail. His men performed their tasks as if their duties had been ingrained in them since birth. The longship caught a strong, advantageous wind, and the square, woolen fabric billowed as the ropes creaked and stretched under pressure. His longship now skated through the water at about three knots, and for the first time since they'd departed the shores of Skúvoy, Gustaf breathed a little easier.

The brisk, salty air blew his hair in all directions and almost whipped his wolf-skin cloak off his shoulders, which reminded him of his Æsa. She hadn't much meat on her bones, and the woolen cloak Didrik had given her was more for disguise than warmth.

Gustaf gestured for Jørgen to take control of the steer board and weaved through the men to where Æsa sat in silence. A few wild strands of hair had escaped her hood, and he tucked them back into place before pulling the cloak tighter at her chin. Still concerned about her warmth, he removed his own wolf-skin cloak and wrapped it around her shoulders.

She barely acknowledged him and stared out across the sea. He cradled her face and forced her to look at him. "Are you all right?" Tears welled in her eyes, and he could feel her body tremble, though he suspected it had nothing to do with the chill in the wind.

"How did Ragnar's ring...?" She couldn't finish her question.

It brought him great discomfort to imagine what she'd endured under Ragnar's control. The thought of that bastard hurting one hair on his Æsa's head infuriated him. "I know not how or why," he muttered solemnly. If anyone knew Ragnar or those he kept company with, it was she. That very concept prompted a whole new range of emotions within him, from torrid jealousy to fuming rage. He tamped them all down and unclenched his fists. "You know Ragnar better than anyone." The taste of that statement was bitter on his tongue, yet he continued. "Was there anyone close to him who would want to avenge him? A brother? A son?"

Æsa flinched and averted her gaze as though he'd struck her. "He had a son…Asmundr."

Though he loathed to know about the men from her past, he encouraged her to speak. "You can tell me. Nothing you say will change how I feel about you, Æsa. Please help me to understand who might be after us."

She closed her eyes and hugged herself, a tear skimming down her cheek. "Asmundr and his father hated each other. He even admitted to me once that he wanted to kill him. I doubt he would bother to avenge him. All he cared about was getting his hands on his father's hoard of buried silver."

"What silver?"

"The silver that—" Æsa stopped herself and gazed at him sympathetically.

Gustaf put two and two together where Ragnar and Harald Fairhair were concerned. "The silver paid to those who killed my father," he finished for her.

"Aye."

Gustaf filled his lungs with a deep breath and took

hold of her hands. "Then it mustn't be Asmundr who's doing this. If anything, Asmundr can obtain all the silver he wants with his father out of the way. I did the man a favor, it seems."

She stared at his thumb brushing along the top of her hand. "Asmundr is dead. Ragnar had him killed."

Gustaf's stomach grew nauseous with each twist and turn of this convoluted story. It pained him to think his Æsa might have played some part in it. Truth be told, he would have rather her end the tale right now with Asmundr dead and no real reason for how Ragnar's ring had come to be in the stream.

As trying as this was to accept, he reminded himself that Æsa's past preceded their relationship, and anything that happened between her and another man would have to be overlooked. It was not easy to imagine her involvement with another man, especially one who'd had a hand in his father's murder.

He regarded her closely and saw her crying. Moved by pity, he pulled her into his arms and held her close, trying to comfort her, though he didn't know what for. Was she deeply saddened by Asmundr's death? Had she once loved him?

As if she'd read his mind, she spat out her feelings in anger. "I hated Asmundr. I hated what he did to me and how it pleased him to see his father walk in on us."

Gustaf's blood scorched through his veins, and his arms tensed around her in a desperate need to protect her.

She buried her face in his neck and sobbed.

"I fought him as best I could, but he was too strong. I pleaded with him to stop, but—"

Gustaf could bear no more. He shushed and rocked her, holding her sobbing body to his chest, glad she couldn't see the fury in his face. He wished the bastard was still alive so he could hunt him down, castrate him on the spot, and stuff his bollocks down his throat.

Unfortunately, the two men who'd brutally defiled Æsa were already food for worms, and the mystery remained for who could possibly be after her now.

He raised his head to the heavens and let the strong winds blow through his hair, cooling his temper. He gentled his hands and cupped her face in his palms. "Do you know where the silver is buried?"

She trembled in his grasp. "I do, but I wasn't supposed to know. I'd overheard Ragnar speak of it."

Realization struck him. "Then someone else knew you eavesdropped, Æsa. Think."

"Asmundr was the only one who'd seen me eavesdropping. Unless…"

"Unless what?"

"Unless he told someone before his father had him killed."

Gustaf clenched his jaw. "You're certain Asmundr is dead?"

Æsa nodded emphatically. "The mercenary Ragnar paid to kill him returned a few moons later, claiming he'd slit his throat and burned the body. As proof, he brought back Asmundr's burnt head in a basket. I didn't look for myself, but Ragnar was…very pleased."

Before Gustaf could stop himself, he wondered if Ragnar had commemorated the death of his son with a celebratory— Nay. He wouldn't finish that thought. It sickened him to think it.

"My lord," Jørgen called from the steer board. "We have stragglers following at a distance."

Gustaf released Æsa and walked toward the rear of the ship. Trailing far behind was a single longship struggling to keep up. Æsa joined them and clutched Gustaf's arm. "Who are they?"

"I suspect the person with whom Asmundr shared your secret before he died. Clearly, you're in search of the buried silver, and they're hoping you'll lead them to it."

"But I'm not," she stated plainly.

"No harm in letting them think otherwise." Gustaf felt the tides turn in his favor. For the time being, he could revel in their foolishness.

"Where *is* the silver?" Snorri asked, prying into the conversation.

An awkward silence hushed across the hull of the ship. Gustaf didn't want to know where his father's blood money was buried or how much had been paid. "Where the silver is buried is not my concern. Our only thoughts should be on how to lead these imbeciles into an ambush."

"You're going to kill them?" Æsa asked as if appalled

by the thought.

"If these men are anything like Ragnar and Asmundr, I can assure you they'll not stop until they have what they want."

Gustaf noticed how pale she turned and pulled her into his arms. He saw a glimpse of her hideous past on her face: the fear, the agony, and the shame she felt all those years. He'd be damned if he let them destroy the woman she'd become. "As long as my heart beats, my dearest Æsa, they will not get to you."

Chapter Twelve

Gustaf wasted no time leaping from his longship into the shallow waters of Skíringssalr's shoreline, just west of the abandoned trading port along Oslofjord. Arms extended, he helped Æsa over the side of the ship, carrying her through the knee-high water to the dry land of the beach. After setting her on her feet, he trudged back through the waves and assisted his men in unloading the few chests of belongings they'd brought with them until the entire ship was bare.

Each man strapped his leather armor, a conical helmet, and a round, colorful shield onto his back. The precision and speed with which these men worked both impressed and frightened Æsa. They were undeniably practiced in the skill of raiding and evading, and she wondered what terror they'd brought to others each time they ran ashore.

"We'll need horses," Gustaf said aloud. He handed Øyven a pouch, which jingled in the transfer of hands. "Find Bryniolfr and purchase as many as you can. Jørgen, take Æsa and see that she prepares for the journey. I'll meet you beyond the forest, in there, out of sight."

"Where are you going, m'lord?" Æsa asked earnestly.

Gustaf gestured with a nod of his head, indicating a group of men who'd taken interest in them distantly beyond the deserted harbor. "To pick a fight."

She immediately grabbed his arm, halting him, but Jørgen came to his aid. "He only means to create a diversion, m'lady. Slow the men who are following us."

"I'll not be long," Gustaf asserted. "Go with Jørgen. I'll meet you in the lowlands. Go."

Although reluctant to obey his command, she did as she was told, and watched him go his separate way.

****

Gustaf eyed the men who gathered at the heart of the port. There were six of them, just enough to give the five at sea a fighting chance.

Upon his approach, they stopped what they were doing and looked him up and down, unimpressed. As if bored, one went so far as to spit on the ground. But Gustaf knew better. They'd seemed to be the kind of men who got aroused by the prospect of a skirmish and would no doubt jump at the chance to whet their swords on the flesh of a few worthless maggots.

"You men look like the arse-end of an inbred swine after a long rut in a whore's swill." Gustaf knew what he'd said made no sense, but these men were too daft to know the difference. His words were only meant to stir the hive.

Their leader squared his shoulders under the insult,

and the rest of the group unsheathed their swords. Gustaf gave a pleasant smile. "Should I assume I have your attention?"

"Oh, you have it," the ugliest one muttered. "Not certain how long I'll let you hold it before I hack you to your knees."

Gustaf threw up his hands. "I wish not to fight you. But I wager *they* would." He turned and pointed to the lonely longship drifting into the estuary.

"And why would I care about the men on that ship when I have a man within reach, more deserving of my sword?"

"Would this be enough to make you care?" Gustaf tossed an overflowing pouch of persuasion at their feet.

The man glanced at the silver that had burst from the sack and back at Gustaf. There was enough there to last these scoundrels through several cold winters, and he knew the big ugly one was sure to yield.

"What have they done to you?" the man asked curiously.

It was not what they'd done to him, but the pain and anguish they'd caused Æsa. No one brought his betrothed to tears and lived to brag about it. "Just make certain they're unable to follow me. And you may use whatever means necessary."

The biggest man gave a harrowing grin, while Gustaf resumed his conditions. "I expect you and your men wouldn't want to do this out in the open. There's too much silver at risk should someone else happen upon you. The forest would be good cover. Follow me."

The leader laughed, and his enthusiasm for the task was a little unnerving. Gustaf picked up the pouch off the ground, handed it to the man, and meandered through the labyrinth of his new venal warriors. With his hired band of mercenaries at his heels, he led them across the lowland beach of the fjord toward the dense forest where his men awaited him.

Gustaf was pleased to see the horses he'd asked for and his trustworthy men making final adjustments to their tack. Æsa's eyes widened when she saw him, but Jørgen nonchalantly held her back from running to meet him. He whispered something to her and went back to tethering his bundles to the rear of the saddle.

"Is she part of the deal?" the leader asked. His barbarous gaze slid over Æsa's curves.

Gustaf froze and threw his arm across the man's chest, halting the man's forward progression. "Whatever you're thinking...put it out of your mind. You'll live longer that way."

His blood boiled over the number of ill-mannered men on this earth, and he ignored the urge to teach them a lesson. Without looking back at the filth behind him, he approached Æsa and tipped her chin up. "Nothing to worry about," he reassured her.

After exchanging a few words with Jørgen, he hoisted Æsa upon his horse and mounted quickly behind her. He took hold of the reins as his horse danced and stamped with the added weight. Once the rest of his men saddled up, he glared at the six miscreant mercenaries still ogling her. "Mark my words, gentlemen. Five men, and not a single one gets past. Are we clear?"

"As you wish," the leader stated, feigning a courteous bow.

Grunting once, Gustaf nudged his heels into his steed's flank and tore off through the woods.

****

Asmundr and his cohorts made quick to pull their boat ashore and follow the men they'd seen disappear into the tree line. Making certain to keep their distance so as not to be spotted, they entered the forest with stealth, their swords unsheathed, their bows nocked.

Asmundr stopped in his tracks and stretched out his hand. His men did the same and peered through the quiet maze of trees, listening for the smallest sound or the slightest movement.

"I know you're in here," Asmundr called into the silence. "Don't be a coward. Show your face like a man."

"Who you calling coward?" a voice erupted before its owner stepped out into the open.

Asmundr noticed the man was as ugly as he was daunting. His face was dirt-ridden and his hair was dark and scraggly, definitely not the man he was following.

Asmundr sighed. "My apologies. I thought you were someone else." He took his first few steps to resume their mission, but five more men appeared from behind the trees, blocking their path. "What is this?"

The ugly man smiled and double-fisted his polished weapon in front of him. It was the only thing unsoiled on his person, which foretold his fondness for the blade. Great care had been taken to forge the iron and even more effort to keep it well whetted. "This would be the end of the road for you," he said.

Asmundr assessed the situation. They were outnumbered only by one. "I believe there is some mistake. I'm traveling with a group of eight men and a beautiful redhead with large tits. I'm certain you saw them come through here."

The man split his lips in a grin, his teeth—what little he had—were rotten and broken. "Oh, I saw the woman." He licked the grime from his mouth as if he'd actually tasted her.

Asmundr's stomach turned. "Then you understand I speak the truth. Now, let us pass."

The ogre shook his head. "See this?" he asked, patting the sack of coins dangling from his belt. "This right here says you lie."

Asmundr realized the extent of the game and laughed. Quietly at first, until the amusement in him could not be withheld. He guffawed so loud it echoed throughout the forest floor. "You're a wise man," he complimented. "And you're correct. I'm not with those men. But I am after the woman."

"Therein lies your problem. I'm not to let you get to her. I'm to see that five men lay dead in this forest, and I aim to please the man who so generously paid me for the task."

"Five men, you say?"

The ugly man nodded.

"Then perhaps I can interest you in a better proposition," Asmundr suggested. "How about I let you keep the coinage, and I only kill your friends. This way, five men shall lay dead on this ground, you'll be five times richer when you take their share of payment from their cold, dead hands."

Asmundr watched as the man's comrades grew nervous with the offer. The one to his left spoke first. "This man is a fool, Vigfuss! A desperate fool! Do not forget the blond warrior with reckless courage who hired us. He'd hunt you down and carve your heart out of your chest for your betrayal. I saw the look in his eyes. He's not a man to underestimate."

"Shut your hole," Vigfuss ordered.

Another spoke up in defense. "Surely, you're not considering this preposterous bargain. Give the word, and we shall make this one pay for his insult."

Asmundr knew he'd struck a chord, so he plucked a little harder, calling the ugly one out by name. "Aye, Vigfuss, what say you? Give the word, and mayhap you'll live. Walk away…and be certain."

Vigfuss mulled it over hard. So hard that eventually his conscience vanished. He sheathed his sword, and walked to stand behind Asmundr and his men.

Disillusioned and enraged, Vigfuss's men lashed out. The cry of war erupted from their lungs, and with swords drawn, they rushed in for the kill. Asmundr drew his sword and pivoted, slashing across the first opponent's back.

Weapons clashing, wills colliding, the men battled in a ferocious struggle for victory. Asmundr's men imposed the most threat as each swing of their blades proved an unparalleled level of accuracy and skill. One by one, the five fell, and the sound of Vigfuss's name spilled from each of their dying lips.

Asmundr staked his sword in the ground and bent at the waist, catching his breath. Spattered with blood, he caught Vigfuss looking back at him. The two exchanged a nod of approval and went their separate ways.

Chapter Thirteen

Gustaf led his men a few kilometers northwest of Skíringssalr along the Numedalslågen River when Jørgen finally rode up alongside him. Moments of silence passed as they trotted abreast. Gustaf could feel his friend's anguish as clearly as if Jørgen were the one sitting astride his horse with him instead of Æsa. "What troubles you, Jørgen?"

"The six we left behind," he stated. "What if they failed? Or worse, took the silver and ran?"

"My concern is for Æsa. Once we get to higher ground, I'll double back and make certain they did as they were paid." Fingernails dug into his arms as Æsa tensed.

"I'll go in your stead," Jørgen insisted as he took notice of Æsa's reaction.

"Take Snorri with you," Gustaf ordered. "And don't get too close. I don't wish to attract any more stragglers. As long as five lay dead, we move on. I'll wait for you at the summit."

Jørgen nodded and reined his horse to the left, acquiring Snorri's assistance. After a few short commands, the two split from the team and galloped out of sight.

****

Æsa settled into the welcomed strength and warmth of Gustaf's body. His muscular thighs braced her in the saddle as they rocked to the slow gait of the horse, and his left arm cradled her against his chest. She should have felt safe in his protective hold, but the thought of someone following them into the wilderness of Norway's terrain kept her on edge.

Gustaf's tense posture didn't help matters either. Though he maintained a credible sense of security with the handful of capable men at his command, he still had suspicions. The way he constantly scanned the surrounding forest with keen eyes and identified every sound he heard over the irregular thumping of his horse's hooves, proved he was just as guarded as she.

She couldn't hold her worries in any longer. "Gustaf, what if Jørgen and Snorri—"

"Shh..." he hushed, giving her body a comforting squeeze. "Unless they stopped to go fishing, they'll return soon."

His jest about his men's shortfall with the "slippery gilled beasts" brought a grin to her lips. He could always make her smile, no matter what troubled her.

After several long hours of climbing the switchbacks on a mountainside, they emerged from the timberline. A vast view of peaks, divided by a narrow inlet of crystalline water under an azure sky, materialized before her eyes. The red and yellow of autumn's reckoning garlanded the foothills below, and her breath caught at seeing the splendor of such a place.

"Where are we?" she asked.

Gustaf pointed at the horizon as the rest of his men came trotting up. "Just beyond those mountains lies the valley in which no one, not even Harald Fairhair, dares to set foot. 'Tis sacred land protected by the spell of the *seiðkona* who lives there, and 'tis where my men's families have taken refuge all these years."

"Are we going there?"

"As soon as we know 'tis safe to venture through."

Æsa's curiosity was as high as the altitude of the ground beneath her. "Does it have a name?"

"*Dal Hinna Dauðu*," Gustaf said, dismounting from behind her. "Its name is not as welcoming as the poetic lilt might imply, for it means Valley of the Dead."

Shivers ran down her spine. Much of chill that had run through her was due to the absence of Gustaf's body heat against her back, but a part of her blamed the ominous place-name and the connotation of death that surrounded it. "Why are you not afraid of such a place, yet the mighty King of Norway is?"

"Because I've not been condemned to the Underworld by the curses of Halldora." Gustaf helped her dismount and began untacking his horse to alleviate some of the weight while the animals grazed. His men did the same and talked low amongst themselves.

"Halldora is a witch?" Æsa inquired further.

"She prefers *seiðkona*, and you'd be best to address her with naught else."

"And Harald Fairhair has been cursed by her?"

"I'm certain he'd like to believe he isn't. But even now that his golden hair has turned white with age, he's yet to test the validity of her spell." Gustaf tossed the last bundle before beginning his story. "'Tis rumored Harald once sought Halldora's counsel because he was eager to know his future as king when he was but a lad. Upon a rune stone, she foretold of a great man, blessed with long flaxen hair, whose domain would expand further than any king before him, should the boy offer a single lock to cast the spell in his favor. Harald, being arrogant and proud of his golden mane, laughed at Halldora, declaring she was naught more than a senseless old shrew with a talent for conjuring up illusions and false prophecies on the face of a fanciful carved stone. He threw his battle-ax at the boulder, and it shattered at her feet. As he turned to leave on his prized stallion, Halldora called upon the powers of the *seiðr* and cast the fragments of stone in a wide circle, encompassing the entire valley and those few standing within it. A few uttered words later, Harald's horse lit up in flames, and he barely escaped with his life before the animal disappeared into ashes. Halldora vowed the same would happen to him should he ever step foot beyond the perimeter again."

"And you believe this?" Æsa asked skeptically as Gustaf heaved his belongings onto his back and carried them over to the base of a tree.

"'Tis not important if I believe it or even you. What matters is that Harald believes it. As long as he fears Halldora, my men's families are safe."

"And what about your family?" she inquired, knowing they lived off the west coast of Ireland. "Aren't you worried about their safety?"

"My brother Dægan ensured their safety years ago. He found a place far away from Harald's reach where they wouldn't need to live in secret."

Gustaf hardly spoke of his family, and Æsa was surprised he mentioned his deceased brother. He was the most generous man she'd ever known, except for when it came to the details about his family. He'd spent so much of his life never speaking of them in order to safeguard their lives that he probably wasn't used to opening up about them.

As she watched him unroll two hides on the ground, she decided not to ask him anything more about his loved ones. "Are we staying here for the night?"

"We are," he said, busying himself in setting up camp. He exchanged words with his men and sent two in search of nourishment, one to tend the horses, and the last to gather wood for a fire.

"What can I do?" Æsa asked.

Gustaf gestured toward the ground where he'd be building a fire. "You can make yourself comfortable."

Æsa crossed her arms as he walked away and caught

sight of Øyven tending to his falcon. In the short time she'd spent with his men, she noticed Øyven often kept to himself, unless Snorri was around to badger him. He stood out as the youngest of the group, his true age of twenty hidden behind a beard of soft scruff. His eyes were kind, and his smile, on the rare occasion when he chose to display it, lit up his youthful appearance.

She remembered Gustaf telling her that Øyven had joined the group only three years ago, after Harald Fairhair had killed his parents. Like her, he'd lost his family at such a young age and was still wandering through life in an aimless fashion. His only companion was that of a bird.

Æsa strolled closer a little at a time until she was able to stroke the muzzle of Øyven's horse. "Gustaf has everyone running around except us. May I stay with you?"

Øyven swapped a glance in her direction and shrugged. "If you'd like." He set the cage down on the ground and untied his belongings from the horse.

Æsa sat down and poked a finger between the tiny bars, stroking the silken feathers along the falcon's wing. "Have you given it a name?"

Øyven joined her on the ground and reached into the cage with a gloved hand. "Her name is Mæva, after my mother." He secured a thin leather strap from his wrist to the bird's leg and rewarded her with a morsel of food. The falcon gobbled it up and stretched its wings, flashing a beautiful array of brown and black feathers.

Æsa petted the bird again, and it tolerated her affection

without snapping.

"It seems she's comfortable with you," Øyven said.

"Mæva is beautiful."

The bird flapped its wings and fluttered about, landing on Æsa's shoulder. At first, she was reluctant to let it perch, but the thick wool of her cloak protected her from its sharp talons.

"Here, give her this."

Øyven produced a small chunk of bait from his pouch, and Æsa gave it to the bird. She couldn't believe she was interacting with such a marvelous, intelligent animal. When the falcon was finished eating, it hopped into the air and returned to Øyven's hand.

"You think you deserve another treat?" Øyven asked.

Æsa laughed, uncertain what she enjoyed more, the fact that the bird learned to hop from person to person in hopes of gaining food, or that Øyven was talking to it like a human. The longer she sat with him and his peregrine, the more comfortable Øyven seemed around her. And before long, they were talking as if they'd been friends since childhood. Æsa enjoyed his company so much that she'd forgotten about the men that were following them and the danger they posed...at least until she saw Gustaf return with an armload of wood and kindling.

She stood and dusted off her bottom. "I should see if Gustaf needs help starting a fire."

"And I should go in search of that waterfall I saw a little ways back before it gets too dark," Øyven said, returning Mæva to her cage.

Once Øyven left, Æsa made her way back to Gustaf, who had just plucked a few long strands of hair from his horse's tail. She watched as he tied them at both ends of a stick to create a makeshift bow and wrapped another stick, sharpened to a point, in the center. He then fashioned a drill, using a rock and a spindle. Using his foot and knee on a flat piece of wood, he held the rock atop the drilling stick and gripped the bow with his right hand. In a delicate balance of downward pressure and moving the bow back and forth, the drill stick spun. It took a long time of sawing the bow, but eventually a black powder formed and a sliver of smoke emitted from his relentless effort. With a tiny hot coal burning on the board, Gustaf carefully transferred it to the tinder of leaves and shredded cedar he'd set at the base of the tented wood. By fanning his hand, the coal ignited a flame, which blazed through the kindling.

On his haunches, Gustaf waited for the wood to catch. When it snapped and crackled under the blaze, he sat back on the hide he'd spread out and slipped a dagger from his boot. With a sandstone in his grasp, he sat in silence, drawing the edge of his blade back and forth against the rock.

Æsa recalled the last instance she'd seen him do this. It was before he'd found the last man who murdered his father, a time when he felt helpless and yet so close to victory. She could only imagine how helpless he felt right now waiting for Jørgen and Snorri's return. Not knowing if they were all right, or if they'd run into trouble was a heavier burden than knowing the truth and making the next calculated move. With Gustaf, everything needed a plan. It was the only way he felt he could keep safe those he cherished.

"You shouldn't punish yourself over your father's death," Æsa said softly as she sat beside him.

Gustaf's hands shook at the mention of his father, and he tried to hide it by increasing the pace of his blade against the stone.

"And you shouldn't punish yourself over me either."

He clutched the dagger and the sanding stone together in both hands and drew in a calming breath. "Dying a thousand deaths in my head to protect you, Æsa, is better than losing you one time in the flesh. I'd never recover if I let anything happen to you. And right now, I'm worried that I put Jørgen and Snorri in danger. I should've circled back instead of them."

Moved by his words, she knelt in front of him and set aside his sharpening implements. His eyes met hers and they stared at one another. Long, heartfelt seconds ticked by as she absorbed the magnitude of his pain. "I'm so sorry for bringing this burden upon you. Yesterday, you were at peace knowing you had fulfilled your duty as a loyal son. And now, you and your men are risking your lives to save me. This is my fault. Not yours."

"Æsa—"

"You can deny all you want what I used to be, but my

dark past is the reason we're in this predicament."

Gustaf clasped her face in his hands. "We all have a moment in our existence that we'd rather erase from our memories. But it matters not what we've failed to do, but what we succeed in doing from those failed moments onward. In my past, I failed to protect my family, and I face that demon every day of my life.

"That being said, our demons do not become us. They are not the bones and flesh of our bodies, nor the substance of our hearts. They are recollections of what used to be and what is no longer. Your demon—or your previous life as a whore, as you like to beat upon my brow—is not who you are inside. Your worth is diminished only by that which you place across your shoulders like a royal cloak. Divest yourself of that burdensome cloak, my dearest Æsa, and you'll understand the depth of my love and the extent to which I will go to protect you." He tipped up her chin that had drooped. "You are worth every risk."

Chapter Fourteen

The warmth of the fire could not match the heat of Gustaf's embrace. He smelled of cedar and smoke, leather and sea salt. Æsa breathed him in and hugged him close, content to rest in her fearless warrior's arms for the rest of her life. He didn't care about her past, and nothing mattered more to her than making him happy. She'd try as best she could to leave her past behind and remember that Gustaf was her future. Together, they'd make it through any hardship or peril the gods threw at them.

Her one hope right now was that Jørgen and Snorri would soon return safely. Like Gustaf, she wouldn't be able to forgive herself if something happened to them.

Eventually, the others filtered back into camp, bringing sweet orange-red cloudberries and plump, savory mushrooms, wood to sustain the fire throughout the night, and even Øyven succeeded in filling several skin pouches with water. They gathered around the fire to eat and passed around stories and jests that helped her get to know Gustaf's fierce warriors as easygoing, jovial men with individual personalities and likable qualities.

Gautr liked to poke fun at Øyven. Not as much as

Snorri, but enough to keep the young man on his guard. Kolskegger had an infectious laugh that could resound over the loud fireside chatter. Beinir was shy like Øyven, but never refrained from talking about his three sons and the wife he couldn't wait to see. Tryggvi, the most handsome of the seven, liked all women in general and kept the men entertained with tales of his most memorable trysts.

Though each one possessed an endearing quality beyond the burly throng of muscles, armor, and beards, none was more appealing than the warrior who sat protectively behind her. From time to time, he'd pop a berry in her mouth and a kiss to her lips, keeping things playful so neither would drown in useless worry over the two who were missing.

At one point, Æsa touched Gustaf's hand and gave a little squeeze, drawing his attention away from the quiet surrounding forest. She looked up at him over her shoulder and smiled. "They must have stopped to fish."

He wrapped his arms tighter round her and laughed, but the sharp snap of a twig breaking caused everyone to stop what they were doing and listen.

Each man already had his hand on a weapon, ready to strike. They waited, their focus bouncing between the alert horses tied to the nearby trees and the surrounding spread of darkness.

Gustaf tapped Æsa on her shoulder and pressed his finger to his lips. With another quick gesture, he and his men rose to their feet, swords in hand, and quietly took their stance in a protective circle.

Æsa's heart beat wildly. The light of the fire made it impossible for her to see anyone that might emerge from the trees. She shook with fear, and the icy chill of possible danger crept under her already goose-pimpled skin.

A bird's call erupted from the silence, followed by Jørgen and Snorri on horseback materializing from the darkness. A collective audible sigh came from the men as they sheathed their weapons. Gustaf eyed the two carefully as they rode up beside him.

"'Tis done," Jørgen uttered in a low voice. "Five."

Gustaf glanced over his shoulder at Æsa, but said nothing to reveal his relief. She watched him praise his loyal duo with discreetness and helped them tend to their horses, while she was left to minister her mixed emotions. She drew comfort in knowing Gustaf had been released from his share of strife in keeping her safe, but she also knew a great number of men lay dead because of it.

Because of her.

****

Gustaf finished looking after his men's horses and noticed Æsa lying down at the fire with his wolf-skin cloak draped atop her body. Since Jørgen and Snorri returned with news of the fallen, she'd barely spoken a word. Women were often too tenderhearted to stomach such violence, and he knew his Æsa was no different.

He was at a loss how to comfort her and decided it was best just to hold her. Curling up behind her, he pulled her close and melted into place along her soft, curvy backside. They had a long few days ahead of them, and they needed to get some much-needed sleep. The amount of time they'd have to spend astride a horse over Norway's rough terrain would prove difficult for even a seasoned rider, much less a woman who wasn't used to the aches and pains of the saddle.

As he closed his eyes, he felt Æsa stir in his arms. He opened them again and found her facing him and covering them both with the wolf-skin cloak. Her dainty fingertips brushed his hair away from his face while the soft globes of her breasts pressed against his chest.

"Sleep well, m'lord."

Her words made him smile. She'd obviously felt the magnitude of his struggles. "I shall sleep better knowing you're no longer in danger. I know 'tis difficult for you to think about what has happened this day, but they were far from innocent men. The ring they planted by the stream was a strong indication of how ruthless they were. They wanted to strike fear into your heart with a powerful message, and they succeeded. I would've been a fool to let them carry out the rest of their wicked plan. Please know that what I did was necessary to protect you."

"I know," she whispered.

He cradled her head in the pocket of his shoulder and stroked her hair. "I'll not let anyone hurt you. Ever. You're safe now. Close your eyes." It took a while for her to completely relax in his arms, but gradually she succumbed to a deep sleep. "I love you," she murmured.

Gustaf fell asleep as well, thinking he could certainly get used to hearing that on her lips every night.

Chapter Fifteen

Morning came like a thief and robbed Æsa of her sweet dream. Her eyes fluttered open upon hearing muffled voices and neighing horses. The blaze that had kept her warm through the night was nothing but a smoldering fire beside her, and the rancid smell of smoke and ash slipped up her nostrils.

As Gustaf had promised, he lay beside her with his heavy arm draped around her waist. He stirred as she did, but his eyes remained closed. She raised her head and saw that his men had had already begun move about. There was a sense of excitement in their movements as each man made preparations to pack. Everyone seemed ready to mount up and journey onward, except Gustaf. He pulled her back down to his chest and snuggled closer, flipping the wolf-skin cloak over their heads.

Æsa giggled at the childlike behavior of her full-grown warrior and stroked his beard. "Hiding beneath your cloak will not trick your men into letting you sleep longer."

"I'm willing to try."

"But they've been so looking forward to going home, Gustaf."

"As have I," he concluded sleepily. "Can we not catch a few more winks?"

Someone kicked Gustaf in his back, causing his eyes to flash open. "On your feet, m'lord, before I jerk you out by your ankles."

Æsa recognized it as Jørgen's voice, and Gustaf peeled the covers back and glared. He didn't proceed to argue with his friend, but he didn't make haste to move either.

"Don't be so grumpy," she said playfully. "He's eager to see his wife after all these years and partake in pleasures you've already obtained." Beneath the cloak, and out of sight, she coiled her hand around him.

"I should warn you, woman," he said in a deep, husky voice. "That part of me is a bit more responsive in the morning." He rolled and pressed an impressive erection between her legs. "Seems a pity to waste it."

Embarrassed that she and Gustaf had become a spectacle, she shoved at his chest but failed to budge him. "M'lord, please."

He dipped his head to her neck and nudged the shell of her ear with the tip of his nose. His whisper came hot against her skin. "It pains me to release you, but I will." With great effort, he pushed himself off her and stood. He held out his hand and helped her to her feet, adding in a whisper, "No one will love you more than I, or as fiercely."

****

Gustaf struggled to relieve himself under the duress of a hard-on, then limped out of the woods to saddle his horse. Æsa also returned from her morning ablutions, and he couldn't help but notice the golden light of the morning sun sparkling in her hair. He watched her comb her fingers through the tangled locks and braid it over her shoulder as she walked. A song was on her lips, a cheery melody he barely heard over the busy work and chatter of his men behind him. But when he listened close, he realized she had a beautiful voice that reminded him of his mother.

As he tacked up his horse and fastened his belongings to the saddle, the sound of her song soothed him in more ways than she'd ever know.

"What can I do to help?" Æsa asked as she rounded his horse and patted its rump.

"You can wear this," he said, pulling out a cloak made of dense brown bear fur from one of his bundles. It was the cloak he'd swiped from Ragnar the day he'd met Æsa and covered her as a considerate gesture to hide the fact that she was naked. It was all he had at the moment, and given they were about to journey through the frigid mountains and valleys of Scandinavia, this was no time for vanity. "Put it over the wool cloak Didrik gave you. You're going to need it."

Her pleasant mood plummeted. She likely held the same distaste for wearing Ragnar's personal garments as he did. "I swear you'll have a new one soon. Made of wolf like mine." He wrapped it around her shoulders as she made no attempt to do it herself. "For now, this will have to do."

He pulled her braid out from underneath the dark sable pelt and smoothed it with the fur. He hated to admit it, but she looked beautiful in it, and flirted with the idea that perhaps a bear's coat would better suit her ivory complexion than the dull gray of a wolf's.

"What are you thinking, m'lord?"

He imagined her sprawled across the soft fur of the animal, her fiery red locks fanning in a halo of silky cinnamon. He clutched the fur beneath her chin and drew her closer, dipping his head to suckle her neck. "I'm thinking how good bear would taste right now."

Æsa giggled, and it delighted him. Far too much. He imprisoned her in an embrace and bit her throat as he growled.

"Either you two mount up, or we're riding ahead of you," Jørgen scolded.

Gustaf looked up with a smile, unwilling to rush his time with Æsa. "Do not let me delay you, my friend. By all means, ride on. I'll be right behind you."

Jørgen kicked his horse onward, and the other six men on horseback followed. Gustaf's horse attempted to go along, but Gustaf grabbed the reins just in time. The animal lunged and circled them, protesting its separation from the herd. It pawed the ground and tossed its head despite Gustaf's effort to calm it.

Irritated with the equine's behavior, he decided it was futile to fight with it. "I suppose we should catch up before this horse lathers himself in a hot sweat." He waited for Æsa to mount and govern the horse before he mounted behind her in one swift leap. As he secured his feet in the stirrups, he wrapped his arms around her body and pulled her tight against his chest. He took control of the reins and turned the dancing horse loose.

****

The hours trickled by slowly, each one melting into the next. The only moments Æsa could vividly recall were the few occasions when a spectacular fjord of deep blue water, sharp cliffs, and colorful native wildflowers in a meadow of green emerged before them. As breathtaking as it was, the ridge of mountains in the background made her realize they still had quite a distance to go.

After the first day, the toll of sitting in a saddle for hours weighed heavily on Æsa's body. The muscles in her back and legs grew stiff, and her bottom felt bruised with the constant bounce of the horse's gait.

Gustaf had warned her that it wouldn't be easy and insisted they'd stop to rest whenever she needed to. But she didn't want to be the one who delayed his men from seeing their families. She knew if it weren't for her, they would've traveled at a quicker pace.

Bearing in mind the many years Gustaf's men had waited for this moment, she endured the pains and aches of their excursion without a word of complaint. And secretly longed for the next break they'd take to water and rest the horses.

By day three, she was exhausted and could barely sit upright. The soreness in her thighs spread to her bones, and she thought her legs might dislocate at the hips. Unable to withstand the torture any longer, she slumped against the solid wall of Gustaf's chest and slung her head back on his shoulder.

"Jørgen," she heard him call out. "We need to stop for the night."

She mumbled something akin to *nay, I'm fine*, but thankfully was ignored. The uncomfortable gait of the horse ceased, and she felt Gustaf shift her weight to one arm. Weak and weary, she feared she'd topple to the ground with no energy to brace herself, but then thought it would be a blessing. At least she'd no longer be subject to the misery of a large hoofed animal between her legs.

She felt Gustaf's grip around her back and behind her knees, lifting her from the unforgiving saddle. The relief of this position washed through her, and her discomfort faded as she lay draped in his arms.

With a thud, his feet hit the ground, and the jolt of his descent ricocheted through her aching spine. She must have groaned for he apologized and hoisted her higher in his embrace. She heard him shout a few orders, and the shuffle of his men's feet close by. Several strides later, her body came to rest on a soft hide spread upon the ground. It felt glorious to be horizontal.

Her hair was brushed from her face, and a tender stroke across her cheek made her lips twitch into a half smile. She'd recognize that touch anywhere.

"Stubborn woman," Gustaf muttered before kissing her softly on the lips.

The warmth of his mouth meeting hers soothed her in ways unimaginable. If she felt any stiffness at all, it quickly dispersed like dandelion fluff on a breeze. The heady scent of worn leather mixed with the woodsy aroma of Gustaf's skin lulled her to sleep.

Chapter Sixteen

The savory smell of roasted meat woke Æsa, but the morning sunlight breaking over the horizon forced her to open her eyes. She saw Gustaf sitting beside her, turning a hare on a spit over the fire.

She made an effort to sit up, and was quickly reminded of the grueling moments she'd spent on horseback. Her muscles cramped, and she moaned, dropping back down.

Gustaf glanced over his shoulder and chuckled. "Still sore, I see."

"Aye."

"I don't think you moved all night after I laid you down."

She smiled. "I dreamed you were snuggled against me."

"'Twas no dream, my dearest Æsa. I was there."

She had no real recollection of it and felt bad that she'd slept right through. "I'm sorry I'm not a seasoned rider."

"I never expected you to be. Here, eat this." He handed her a chunk of charred meat that steamed in the brisk air. "'Twill help you regain your strength."

She took one bite and hummed with satisfaction. It had been a long time since she'd eaten anything this substantial. A person could last only so long on wild berries and mushrooms, as compared to the filling benefits of animal protein, and she wasted no time gobbling it up.

"You still have your appetite," Gustaf jested, handing her another.

As she finished the second piece, she heard a lively sound of hoots and hollers in the distance. "Where are the others?"

"We are but a short ride from our destination, and the men found a waterfall when we went hunting this morning. They're freshening up before they greet their women."

She glanced over herself, feeling less than presentable. This was an important day for Gustaf's men, and showing up tattered, weak, and smelling of horse was not the first impression she wanted to deliver. "I'd like to clean up as well."

"I intend for us to do so, but I think 'tis best to wait until they are through. You know what happens when grown men frolic in water."

"Actually, I don't," she confessed.

He wagged his brow. "They turn into devious boys and end up dunking everything in sight."

Æsa remembered how Gustaf had thrown her into the cold stream upon his return to the Faroes. "No worse than you, I'd imagine."

Gustaf's hearty laughter echoed around her, and it was

a rarity she came to cherish. With their troubles far behind them, she hoped it would be a common occurrence, especially after they became husband and wife. As she longed to be the source of his joy for the rest of his days and imagined giving him the sons he'd always wanted, their conversation on Skúvoy circled back into her thoughts.

"I want to fill our home with many sons."
"And daughters?"
"Aye, and daughters. I can only hope they resemble your beauty and speak with fire on their tongues."
"And if they do not?"
"I shall love them anyway, for they'll come from your womb."

She envisioned Gustaf cradling a babe in his arms and teaching the youngster all there was to know about the new world he'd been born into. That was, if she could provide him a child at all. Given that no man's seed from her sordid past had ever taken root, she worried her womb was barren.

"What are you thinking?"

His voice broke apart her painful thoughts, and she struggled to fabricate a credible answer to his question. "I was thinking of us, and you as a father. I'm eager to be your wife and the mother of your children."

Gustaf tipped his head in surprise. "Children? From where did that thought come?"

Another bout of spirited shouts erupted, followed by a

considerable splash as if some poor fool had hit the water. His question had been asked and answered.

"It would bring me great pleasure to birth many sons for you."

"Many sons?" Gustaf asked as he considered the thought. "You do realize I'm a man of mature age. 'Twould require a considerable amount of lovemaking to produce many sons."

"I'm willing if you are," Æsa stated.

Gustaf scooted closer and inclined his body over hers, bracing his weight on one elbow. His dark blond hair fell over his shoulder and hugged the sharp angle of his jaw shadowed with scruff. "I'm always willing. For the rest of my life, I'll do whatever it takes to ensure your happiness. As my wife, you'll not want for anything. What you desire, I will provide."

"I desire only you, m'lord. To marry you and love you until I take my last breath."

He bent to kiss her, but stopped midway. "Would it disappoint you if we waited to marry until we returned to Inishmore?"

The warmth of his breath across her lips caressed her starved skin. The blue of his eyes sparkled like the depths of the crystal sea. It still seemed hard to fathom that this beautiful man was all hers. "You could never disappoint me, Gustaf. I've been without a family for so long that knowing you'd rather share our union amongst yours is an honor."

His smile stroked her all the way to her soul, and his kiss singed her entire body, making her fully aware of how hard her heart beat in her chest. She arched into him, craving his touch like a delicate flower in desperate need of warm sunlight.

He pulled sharply out of the kiss. "We can't do this. We're not alone. My men."

His clipped words resounded in her head. "Then let's go where we *will* be alone."

Chapter Seventeen

Asmundr swiped his hand across his mouth and wiped away the horrid taste of jealousy. From a distance, he'd watched Æsa strip to nothing and lure the blond giant to the edge of the stream, offering her favors to him like the whore she was. His view from the top of a densely covered hillock allowed him the pleasure of keeping a close eye on them, though he'd rather not have seen them fornicate like intimate lovers. It sickened him to know she favored this worthless knave over what he had to offer.

Fickle bitch.

She could have been treated like a princess under his care, instead of a groveling concubine. And for what? A hoard of buried silver that she'd have to split nine ways? Had she trusted in him, she could have had so much more.

His bollocks ached as he watched Æsa moan in ecstasy beneath the deep, hard thrusts of another man. Her wanton behavior wore his tolerance thin, and he vowed he'd soon punish her the way she deserved. The way *he* deserved for all he'd sacrificed for her in the past.

Asmundr continued to spy on her as she and the rutting warrior bathed in the water. He plotted his revenge down to the last detail of the warrior's death and Æsa's torture, then left when he'd had enough of watching them kiss.

He strode down the hill to where his loyal mounted men waited, and scaled his own horse in exasperation. "They are moving on," he proclaimed, clutching his reins in an embittered fist. "But as of right now, they still outnumber us. We'd be fools to try anything prematurely." He rotated his father's ring around his finger and stewed in his thoughts. "Fortunately for us, she has one of them under her spell. Soon he'll grow careless, and when he does, we'll strike."

****

Gustaf barely noticed the stark beauty of Lake Mjøsa or the majestic, snow-capped mountains in the distance. The only thing that held his attention was the slow, swaying gait of the horse that rocked Æsa's sumptuous body against his. Memories of their recent passionate endeavor coupled with the feel of his hips cradling her soft round bottom tormented him until he could bear it no longer.

He leapt off the side of the horse and landed on the ground with a thud. An arctic autumn breeze funneled through the valley, and he froze in his tracks. A ring of shattered rune stones from Halldora's ancient spell lay at his feet, encircling an area of dense forest.

"M'lord," Jørgen announced. "We're here. We're about

to cross over into the Valley of the Dead."

Another haunting wind kicked up around them, warning of unnatural forces afoot amid a ghostly low-lying fog adrift along the forest floor. Gustaf stepped over the threshold, careful not to disturb the edging of rocks as he led Æsa and his horse through. He breathed a sigh of relief when his men also reached the other side unscathed, but he knew better than to think their presence was welcomed.

"We are not alone," Jørgen warned.

Gustaf unsheathed his sword and turned to Æsa. He motioned for her to dismount and assisted her on the way down, guarding her with his body. "Stay close to the horse," he whispered, handing her the reins. He removed the shield strapped to his back and secured it in his left hand. "Keep your head down."

He circled the animal and stalked toward the front of the group. The wind picked up, and the horses nickered nervously. As the rest of the men unsheathed their swords, Gustaf approached the forest one step at a time.

"Halt!" a deep male voice called out from within the whistling timbers. "You're on sacred land, and unless you wish to take your last breath where you stand, I suggest you turn around and return from whence you came."

Gustaf gripped his sword a little tighter. "We've come a long way, and we mean no harm to the people you safeguard within these borders."

"State your name and your purpose," the voice demanded.

Jørgen and Gustaf exchanged uneasy glances. "I'm Gustaf, son of Rælik, and these are my men. Their families are protected here, and we wish to see them."

A long span of silence elapsed after he spoke. The hairs on the back of Gustaf's neck stood up and his stomach hardened. Nausea was close at hand. Here, in this enchanted place, he was a vulnerable target no matter how well he fortified himself with sword and shield. He had no experience negotiating with those whose powers extended beyond the realm of natural forces. Whether real or hoax, he wasn't about to test the power of black magic or disrespect the supernatural with undue impatience. He'd stand like a statue until the sun set if he had to.

"There is no one here by that name," the voice said finally.

"'Tis true," Gustaf said. "You wouldn't recognize the name Rælik as you sound too young to remember. Halldora would recall my name. Perhaps you might send for her."

"And leave my post unguarded? Think again."

Gustaf reined in his irritation. "Might we at least possess the knowledge of your name before we're turned away?"

"I'm Ketill, son of Jørgen. Now be gone."

Gustaf moved, only to look at his friend. He could see Jørgen contending with the unfamiliar sound of his grown son's voice, and the realization that he failed to recognize it. Jørgen's face fell in shame and unshed tears welled in his eyes.

"Unless you wish to run your own father through, Ketill," Gustaf said on behalf of his friend who was overwrought with emotion, "I suggest you lay down your weapons and greet him as a son should."

"My father is dead."

Jørgen clutched his heart and choked back a sob. "I left when you were but a lad of four. And you would be twenty and seven now. Your brother, Ulfr, would be twenty and five. Is he there with you?"

Again, silence followed, save for the blustery wind that howled in their ears. Jørgen's desperation to convince his eldest son of his identity climbed as he spouted things only a father and husband would know.

"Your mother's name is Gunnhildr. She has a crooked finger on her right hand because she punched the horse that nearly toppled you when you were two. She didn't tell me so it could be splinted. Ulfr has a scar under his left eye where you struck him with the wooden sword your uncle fashioned for you on your birthday. A fortnight before I left, I strung bows for you and your brother, asking you both to protect your mother in my absence. I suspect they are nocked with arrows pointed at my weary heart as we speak... Not a day has gone by that I've not thought of the family I left behind." Jørgen kicked his leg over the horse's neck and slid out of the saddle, throwing aside his weapon and shield. Divested of arms, he outstretched his hands. "Please come forward, and let me see the fine young men you've grown into. Please...I need to see you. Do not send me away, I beg you. I've come home." His voice cracked as he repeated his last words. "Your father has come home."

Out of the forest and through the gray mist rode a tall, strapping lad with broad shoulders and stout legs on an equally impressive black gelding. In his grasp, he held careful aim on Jørgen's heart with a longbow. At his hip was a broadsword and a multitude of daggers sheathed along his belt. Garbed in a wolf-skin cloak and knee-high fur-lined boots, he was a warrior who would make any father proud.

The young man circled Jørgen on the horse. Heavy hooves stamped the ground as he stared with guarded, menacing eyes. From behind him, another rode out on horseback, younger in age but no less daunting. Like his brother, he employed the tactic of intimidation as he approached and affixed his gaze on the father he thought dead.

Gustaf held his position, toggling between Jørgen and the two warriors who surrounded him. Twenty-three years of pent-up pain, elation, and relief erupted from Jørgen, and he dropped to his knees at the sight of his two brave sons who'd grown into full-fledged, fearless champions.

The two men lowered their weapons and dismounted, running to Jørgen's aid and helping him to his feet.

"Is it really you, Father?" Ketill asked, studying a stranger's face for a sign of familiarity.

Tears of joy ran down Jørgen's cheeks as he felt the touch of his own flesh and blood on his cheeks, and looked into the two pairs of eyes akin to his own. There was no denying he sired the two handsome lads at his side. "Of course, 'tis I. Look at me." He grabbed each of his sons' napes and pulled them into a firm, manly hug. "Look at how you have grown! Odin's blood, your mother feeds you well."

They traded hearty embraces over gales of excited laughter. It was a beautiful sound to hear mature men rejoice, for it wasn't a common occurrence amongst Gustaf's tight band of mercenaries. He'd never seen Jørgen weep with joy, and he doubted he'd ever see it again.

Gustaf sheathed his sword and glanced at Æsa. She too fell into tears over the emotional, long-awaited reunion between father and sons.

One by one, Gustaf's men sheathed their weapons and dismounted to join in on the merriment. Introductions and fervent embraces abounded as everyone reacquainted themselves with the two warriors they once knew as rowdy boys. Everyone save for Øyven, who'd come into the group at a later date, and Æsa.

"And this," Jørgen commenced, holding out his upturned hand in Gustaf's direction, "is the great son of Rælik. Gustaf, my most loyal friend and lord."

Gustaf could barely look them in the eye, for he was the very reason they'd been separated from their father for nigh a quarter of a century. "Forgive me for keeping your father away so long."

Ketill and Ulfr dropped to their knees before him and

hung their heads in humble gratitude. "You've brought our father back from the dead," Ketill said. "We're forever indebted to you."

Gustaf gazed upon the two lads kneeling at his feet. Their blind servitude reminded him of the unconditional fealty Jørgen had provided him all these years. "On your feet. Both of you." He then bowed his head and stood before Jørgen. "I should be kneeling before you, my friend. Your sacrifice goes beyond what any man should be expected to offer."

Jørgen marched forward and stood eye to eye with Gustaf. "I have no regrets, m'lord. I would serve you again, if necessary."

Gustaf had no doubt. But Jørgen's days of being without his loved ones were over, and it gave him greater pleasure to know they could celebrate this occasion together. He flung his arm around his friend's shoulder and puffed out his chest. "If you insist upon serving me, Jørgen, a large drinking horn full of mead would suit me just fine."

A roar of vigorous shouts erupted as every man came to the same conclusion.

"What are we waiting for, men?" Jørgen proclaimed with his fist in the air. "Let's go home!"

Snorri mounted his horse before anyone else and reared it high in the air. "May the mead run aplenty and the women run amok!"

Chapter Eighteen

It was a grand day to be among those who'd finally made it home to their families and friends. The joyful noise of everyone's surprise carried like squawking seagulls throughout the valley. Not one could contain themselves as villagers young and old came bustling out of their longhouses and realized their husbands, brothers, and fathers were alive.

Æsa understood well the elation that swelled in their hearts, for not long ago she'd felt the same upon Gustaf's homecoming. She remembered how she nearly tripped on her own two feet to get to him, and how strong and comforting his embrace was as he swung her around.

This was a special day for all.

As she, Gustaf, and his men were ushered toward a large wooden building in the center of many surrounding longhouses, her focus was directed to Ketill and Ulfr. They trotted their horses in a circle, rallying the others.

Ketill, being the more dominant, announced a plan. "We should hunt together as brothers united. Who's with me? Father?"

Jørgen lifted his head from the haven of his wife's

neck, holding fast to her body. "You'll have to forgive me, son. I have other intentions this day."

Suggestive remarks and jests flew about with no remorse. Ulfr even covered his ears as insinuations were made about his parents.

"Surely not every man is as weak as my father." Ketill winked at Jørgen and then searched the faces of the many able-bodied men surrounding him. "Who among you still gets hard with the thrill of a hunt?"

Snorri piped up first. "That would be me." He trotted alongside Ulfr and beckoned his chieftain. "What say you, Gustaf?"

To Æsa's dismay, Gustaf didn't think twice. He grabbed a firm hold of mane and kicked his leg up over the horse. "Count me in," he shouted.

Everything happened so quickly, and before she realized what was happening, Gustaf bent at the waist, clasped her face with both hands, kissed her hard, and left her behind in a whole mass of strangers. There wasn't a single person she recognized as she searched the joyous people surrounding her. They hopped and laughed and danced in a circle, celebrating without a care in the world.

She staggered, feeling dizzy. Overwhelmed. Flushed and nauseated. She clutched her stomach and, with her other hand, reached for stability. A woman steadied her by the elbow, but her vision blurred.

"Are you all right?" Æsa heard her say over the commotion of the people. "You don't look well. Perhaps, you're spent from the long journey."

Æsa nodded and squeezed the woman's hand tighter. A strong arm from behind her wrapped around her waist and pulled her against a firm chest. A man's chest, muscled and warm.

"I'll watch over her." The familiar voice belonged to Øyven, and Æsa was glad. She caught a glimpse of his youthful face, his soft beard, and his quiet concern as he asked the question, "Might there be a stable for my horse?" and then she fainted.

****

Æsa came to from the potent smell of fresh manure and old hay. She swallowed back the urge to gag, and bolted upright. Seeing that she sat in the middle of a spacious barn, she took this moment to collect herself. Though she could still hear the enthusiasm of the celebrating outside, she found comfort in the solitude provided here.

As she opened her mouth to call Øyven's name, a gray-haired woman of tiny build entered the barn. "He'll be along in just a while," she said in the frailest of voices. "He's watering his horse with my granddaughter."

"Who is?" Æsa asked.

"Øyven," the woman answered matter-of-factly. "That's whose name you were going to call out for, is it not?"

The strange woman stood no taller than an adolescent girl, but the wrinkles creasing her face proved her age. She had a slow, unsteady gait that demonstrated the strength in her bones had failed long before the sharpness of her mind, and the crooked smile fixed on her lips prefaced that she harbored no resentment toward the hardships life had dealt her.

She shuffled forward and sat on a bench beside Æsa, patting it. "Come now. Don't be afraid."

Æsa joined the elderly woman on the bench, but still felt uneasy with her keen sense of foresight. Long, bony fingers reached for hers and took hold. The chill of the woman's skin presaged a whole host of mixed emotions, and before Æsa could ask about Gustaf's whereabouts, the old woman spoke again.

"He went hunting, remember?" The woman snapped her fingers in front of her nose. "Did you fall and hit you head perhaps?"

Æsa's eyes widened in disbelief. "No, I didn't. And can you really hear my thoughts?"

"I hear everything. As soon as one steps foot within the boundary of the rune stones, their thoughts are mine. 'Tis a curse at times, as there are some people's thoughts I'd rather not hear at all."

The woman turned her head and regarded Øyven, who'd walked into the barn and froze at the sight of her. He stood as a silhouette in the shadows, holding fast to his horse's bridle in one hand and his birdcage in the other.

The old woman spoke before Øyven could ascertain her name or her purpose.

"I heard your thoughts too, young man." A gray brow lifted above her harsh gaze despite the implication of amusement in her smile. "That's my granddaughter you were with. Shame on you."

Øyven cleared his throat and led his horse into a stall, no doubt skeptical of the woman's ability to hear his thoughts as she'd claimed.

"You can question my talents all you'd like, Øyven, but if you so much as look at Helga again the way you did when she bent to fetch a bucket of water from the lake, I'll string you up by your ears. You'd do best to treat her with more respect. Like you treat Æsa, here."

Øyven paused as he shut and latched the wooden gate on the stall, then turned to say something. But the old woman stopped him.

"I've heard enough. Why don't you step outside with your falcon and let it stretch its wings. Æsa will be fine under my charge." She chuckled softly and patted Æsa's knee. "He's unsettled by leaving you alone with me. Perhaps he'd feel better if it came from you."

Æsa gave Øyven a look of pity. "'Tis all right. I'll be well. I promise."

"Are you certain?" Øyven asked.

The old woman waved her hands in front of her, shooing him. "Go. Take care of your bird. And see to Helga for me. Rest assured, I've no qualms about you pursuing her as long as you mind your manners. Go beyond that, and I'll have to slap you."

Reluctantly, Øyven exited the barn, and Æsa wished she'd begged him not to leave her alone with the eccentric old witch. As quickly as she thought it, she tried to erase it, fearing the woman might have already heard it.

"Who are you?" Æsa asked instead.

"I'm Halldora, the condemned heretic. Or the guardian of Dal Hinna Dauðu—whichever you favor. I prefer the latter."

Æsa recalled the story Gustaf had told her about Harald Fairhair and his horse that lit up in flames. "Is it true you cursed the King of Norway?"

The grin on the old woman's face pushed more wrinkles around her eyes. "The truth lies within the circle of the rune stones. Unless the old bastard dares to cross it, we may never know. Yet, 'tis with great certainty that I can attest to the proud king's trepidation. To date, he has failed to muster enough courage for such an attempt, and I doubt he ever will as long as there is breath in me. 'Tis my only hope that I outlive the old worm."

"The spell dies with you?" Æsa asked.

"Naught is forever, child. That is the will of the gods." Halldora reached up with a trembling hand and stroked Æsa's hair. "And just like curses that fade with time, so will your fears about a barren womb."

"You know about that?" Æsa asked.

Halldora took her hand and closed her eyes as if she

were making an assessment through physical contact. Then she smiled and rocked to a rhythm only she seemed to hear. "Make no mistake. You're with child right now." She turned her ear toward Æsa's body and listened. "'Tis a boy. His heartbeat is strong and steady, like his father's."

Æsa wanted to cry out and rejoice in this miracle, but her suspicions wouldn't let her. "How can this be?"

Halldora's eyes shot open. "I assume you're not so naïve as to question the intimate particulars of how a child comes to be in this world. You've lain with the mighty warrior, aye?"

Æsa thought back to days she spent with Gustaf holed up in the little cottage he provided her before he left to save his family from Gunnar Haveloksen. They'd made love countless times… But then her thoughts shot back to the day she'd met Gustaf, and the fact that she'd been with Ragnar.

"Fear not, my child," Halldora reassured her. "The babe does not belong to that wicked man." She took Æsa's hands and placed them on her belly not yet showing signs of pregnancy. "Relish this moment, child. The gods have given you a gift, an answer to the prayer you've lifted to them. Gustaf's heir grows in your womb."

Æsa hugged her stomach, imagining the son that she'd bear in the spring. "I can't wait to tell Gustaf the news." She stood with excitement but remembered he'd gone out on a hunting expedition.

Halldora pulled her back down to the bench and held

her hand tightly. She closed her eyes and channeled her foresight over the distant men who hunted in the forest. "It pains Gustaf to be away from you, and he feels remorse for leaving you behind in haste. He thinks this even as he takes aim upon a massive brown bear eating berries—"

"A bear?"

Halldora smiled and shushed her as if her concern would distract Gustaf from making the kill. "Its hide is what he wants. He has aspirations of making you a bear cloak because he loathes the one you're wearing now." Halldora peeked out of one bulging eyeball to gaze at the fur draped around Æsa's shoulders and lowered her lid again to resume her vision. "I believe the man hates Ragnar more than you do. Ulfr has agreed to tan the hide, but 'tis a surprise—so pretend astonishment when Gustaf gives it to you."

Æsa tried to appreciate the account of Gustaf's thoughts and the knowledge she'd been given about a new cloak, but she was more concerned that he was face-to-face with a dangerous beast.

"Oh my," Halldora gasped.

Æsa watched as the seidkona's face shriveled up with apprehension. "What is it? What do you see?"

"The bear smells Gustaf and 'tis looking right at him. He's walking around a tree to get a better view."

"Gustaf or the bear?"

"Gustaf," Halldora answered. "He needs to get closer to ensure a swift kill. He is not as skilled with the bow as

Jørgen."

Æsa bit down hard on her lip to keep from screaming. She suddenly wasn't so fond of Halldora's visions.

"He has his aim but doesn't release the arrow. The other men are taunting the animal as they ride around it. They are working in unison to anger the bear, to get it to stand on its hind legs. Gustaf is drawing near."

"Nay!"

"Hush, child. He knows what he's doing. This is not his first kill."

Æsa didn't care if it was his five-hundredth kill. She knew a bear could maul a man with one swipe of its mighty paw. Even if Gustaf dodged that gruesome demise, the bear was capable of running him down on foot. Unless Gustaf pierced the animal's heart on the first shot, her courageous warrior was as good as dead.

Æsa squeezed the old woman's hands, waiting with bated breath for the outcome. Halldora's eyes slowly opened and gazed into hers, no emotion registering. She stared as if something bad had happened, and she had no way of knowing how to share the horrible news. The wait became intolerable.

Æsa let go of Halldora's hands and gripped her by the arms. She shook the old woman until she broke the trance. Halldora blinked and leapt back into her own thoughts. "Please, Halldora! Tell me. Is Gustaf all right?"

A smile curved her thin lips. "'Tis said that the paws and thighs of a bear are the sweetest meat. I suspect we shall come to form our own opinion soon enough with the feast that is to come. I hope you like bear."

Chapter Nineteen

Gustaf trotted through the forest in front of the men who were carrying their praises of the valiant hunt on their lips. Ulfr and Ketill brought up the rear, dragging the bear on a makeshift sled behind their horses. The bear was a massive animal, a lone male that had been stocking up on reserves for his upcoming winter's nap just moments before an arrow pierced its heart. Its carcass would yield more than enough meat for a feast and quite a heroic tale about its mighty fall to boot.

The men would spend the rest of the evening in the mead hall, drinking, feasting, and taking turns telling the story to the entire village. It was customary to hear each man try to outdo his fellow chronicler in a dramatic oration, one that boasted both great detail and enthusiasm.

There was only one who could put the best narrators in their place, and that was Gustaf's brother Dægan. He could seize everyone's interest with a single introduction and hold their undying attention with the grandest of ease. Sometimes he brought listeners to tears, others to laughter. But it was his authoritative poetic style that made his fireside tales memorable.

In reminiscing upon his brother's talent, Gustaf realized he'd never get the privilege of hearing Dægan's commanding voice again. He was gone, just like so many others in his family.

The thought brought him great sadness and he pushed it out of his head. Dægan was probably drinking in Valhalla with his father, uncles, and Eirik, and he should be proud. He could only hope he too would be chosen by Odin upon his death and join his brothers in arms in the Great Hall.

As the villagers emerged from the mead hall, Gustaf searched their faces, looking for Æsa. Though he didn't find her amongst the fuss of the congregating people, he caught a small boy staring at him in awe. He dismounted his horse and approached the young child.

"Did you slay the bear?" the lad asked as he looked up at Gustaf.

Gustaf squatted to his level. "We all did. And one day," he added, tousling the boy's hair, "you will too."

The boy smiled at the prospect of joining the hunt in his later years, and he reminded Gustaf of his nephews on Inishmore, eager to please their elders, ready to pounce on an adventure, and so full of mischief. He winked at the lad, then stood as he glanced again over the collected villagers.

"Are you looking for the pretty woman who can braid fire down her back?"

He smiled at the boy's description of his Æsa's hair. "Indeed, I am. Do you know where I might find her?"

"She's in the field with the man who talks to birds," he

said, pointing to the meadow. "I think she likes him."

Gustaf tried to ward off the unexpected jealousy that arose over Øyven. "Oh? And what makes you think that?"

"Because he oftentimes makes her giggle. Mama says when a girl laughs, she's happy. But when a girl giggles, she's happy in love."

Gustaf didn't mean to be envious of a warrior he trusted with his life. It was childish, he knew, but nonetheless, he was. He stood and gazed at Æsa and Øyven, who were occupying their time training the falcon. Øyven was about twenty paces from Æsa in the open field, and the bird was flying between the two and landing on the leather-gloved hand of whichever person had the bait. Another girl, also a redhead whom Gustaf didn't recognize, stood beside Øyven, fawning and giggling for his attention.

"As you can see, my granddaughter holds Øyven's fancy. Not your Æsa."

Gustaf recognized the familiar voice before he turned and laid eyes on its owner. "Halldora." He bowed slightly in respect. "In my head again, I see."

"As of late, 'tis not a nice place to be." Halldora took him by the crook of his arm and led him away from the others, his horse trailing behind them. "You needn't concern yourself with Øyven. He's not a threat to you, unlike your own mulish pride."

Gustaf was glad Halldora pulled him away from the group before chastising him for the thoughts he'd had. What he didn't like was being browbeaten by an elderly woman one-third his size. Still, he tolerated and respected Halldora. He owed her that much after all the years she'd spent protecting his men's families.

"I assume you have acquainted yourself with Æsa."

"She's lovely," Halldora replied. "And a good match for you, though you don't deserve her."

"You certainly enjoy cutting me down to size."

Halldora chuckled innocently. "'Tis an easy task with one so haughty."

"I'm not haughty, Halldora."

"Aye, you are. And soon, you'll be happier than you've ever been."

He gave her a stern look from the corner of his eye. "You speak as though you know something I do not."

"What I know is not my place to say."

Gustaf shook his head and scoffed. "You and your riddles. I should have known better than to think you'd be forthcoming where others' private thoughts are concerned."

"Trust me, warrior. You'll be glad of what you hear, and that it came from Æsa's lips. Not mine."

It drove Gustaf crazy that she knew every person's innermost thoughts. She was like a priest from the new Christian religion who swore to keep all confessions secret, but unlike the holy men, she had no qualms about boasting of her mystic powers.

He placed his hand over the frail, bony fingers that held tight to his bicep. "I know you mean well, Halldora, but I grow tired of talking in circles with you. Now, if you'll pardon me, I aim to strike up a real conversation with a woman who doesn't know my every word before it falls from my lips." He regarded her carefully as he gently patted her knuckles. "I thank you for keeping watch over Æsa, even if 'twas only to meddle."

"The pleasure was all mine, oh great son of Rælik."

Gustaf laughed, then mounted his horse. "Stay out of my head, *seiðkona*."

"What would be the fun in that?"

Gustaf raised his brows for extra measure. "I mean it, Halldora."

Chapter Twenty

Æsa's heart skipped a beat when she heard the pounding of Gustaf's galloping horse across the meadow. She wanted to run up and throw her arms around his neck, but Øyven's falcon perched on her gloved hand. She fed the bird a treat and watched as Gustaf came to a skidding halt in front of her. Like her, he was beaming.

His horse danced, unwilling to stand still, so he reined the horse to walk in a circle around her. Bowing deeply over the saddle, he held her gaze. "My lady," he said humbly.

"My lord," Æsa replied in the same jovial manner. It occurred to her that he was very proud of his successful hunt because he'd not only provided his men and their families with ample food, he'd soon have a tanned bearskin cloak to give her as he'd once promised. Though she'd pretend not to know and then feign surprise after he gave it to her, she couldn't wait to give Gustaf the gift of her news.

As Øyven and Helga walked up, she decided she'd hold it a little while longer until they were alone. By this time, Gustaf was able to give his horse freedom to graze. He leaned forward and rested his elbow on the pommel of the saddle. "I appreciate you keeping Æsa company in my absence, Øyven."

"'Twas no trouble, m'lord. Æsa has been a great help in training Mæva."

Æsa held out her hand to Øyven and transferred the falcon to his wrist. "I hope you'll allow me the honor of assisting you again with her lessons on the morrow."

Øyven smiled. "I would like that very much. It seems she's quick to learn when you're near."

Æsa couldn't agree more. The young bird, though barely a *passager*, expressed an uncanny sense of being manned and lured without prior rigorous schooling.

"Perhaps tomorrow we can hack her," Øyven suggested. When Æsa's eyes bulged wide, he jiggled the leather strip fastened around the bird's leg and added, "That means to give her liberty to fly." Everyone laughed, and Æsa breathed a sigh of relief as Øyven looked at Gustaf like he'd done many times before for permission. "Would that be possible, m'lord?"

Gustaf nodded. "I suspect I can occupy my time tomorrow while the two of you tend to the bird's training. In the meantime, I request the honor of my betrothed." He held out his hand and lowered a heated gaze at Æsa. "Will you ride with me?"

Æsa could no more refuse his invitation than she could stop her heart from beating. In the instant she took his hand, he hoisted her up behind him in the saddle. He governed the horse while she wrapped her arms around his waist and pulled herself against his back. She'd almost forgotten how large Gustaf was until she tried to link her hands together at his navel. Between the mass of muscle in his torso and the thickness of the wolf-skin cloak draping down his back, her arms barely reached.

"M'lord," Øyven interjected. "You'll be back in time for the feast, I assume."

"I wouldn't miss it," Gustaf said as he restrained the horse that pranced beneath him. "But a word of advice now that you'll be alone with Helga, Halldora's granddaughter…" He inclined his head and winked. "You're never truly alone."

Øyven laughed under his breath. "I'm well aware of Halldora's…gifts."

Gustaf found Øyven's clever modification of his words amusing. "You can change your words all you like. Halldora still knows what goes unspoken."

"Duly noted, m'lord."

****

Gustaf rode out along the banks of the crystalline lake as distantly as he could to escape the many villagers who inhabited the secret valley and to be alone with his beautiful betrothed. He even went so far as the ring of scattered, spellbound rune stones in order escape a particularly nosey old woman who loved to take up permanent residence in his head.

He dismounted and carefully guided his horse across the boundary, looking downward to ensure its hooves didn't disturb a single stone.

"Halldora unravels you no end, doesn't she?"

Gustaf took a deep breath and spoke openly about his feelings now that he was safe from the witch's intrusion. "She is one woman I'd want on my side in battle, but I care little for the battle she likes to wage when I know she's in my head."

He tied the horse to a tree limb, then came for Æsa. He took hold of her waist and pulled her off the horse into his arms. He held her tightly, burying his face in her hair and breathing in the potent aroma of sweet primrose. He missed touching her, tasting her, and before he realized, he seized her mouth in a hard, emphatic kiss.

He swept his tongue past her lips and savored the feel of her tongue entangled with his. All the blood from his brain rushed to his groin, and he knew if he didn't have her soon, he'd burst.

He gripped the material of her tunic at her thighs and lifted her skirts. Creamy smooth skin met hard, coarse knuckles, and they fell to their knees in a frenzy of kisses as they stripped each other naked.

Chapter Twenty-one

Making love with Gustaf was always good, but this time proved to be more special than all the rest. There was an unmistakable purpose in his touch, as though he were reverently worshipping every curve and swell of her body. Each thrust was slow and methodical, tender and compassionate. And now, as they coupled in sweet rapture at the base of an old oak tree, Æsa memorized this moment.

The bright blue lake of Mjøsa stretched out for miles before them beneath a twilight sky. The steep mountains of Jotunheimen stood guard to the northwest, and the serenade of night insects mingled with the lulling cadence of Gustaf's heartbeat in her ears.

She snuggled against him, finding complete solace in lying atop his chest in a cocoon of wolf and bear fur. She stroked her hand over the hard bulge of chest muscle and down his flat stomach, tracing a playful finger through the strip of dark blond hair below his navel.

Gustaf captured her wrist and pulled it away before she dipped lower. "You're tickling me."

"You do not like to be tickled?" she asked.

He glanced at her smiling lazily up at him. "I do not like to be tormented."

"Release my hand, and I shall end your torment," Æsa dared.

Gustaf chuckled and rolled onto her, trapping her beneath the weight of his heavy body. "My mind is ready and willing, but other parts of me are not equipped for such a feat. There're some things that require patience, my dearest Æsa."

Long quiet moments passed. Gustaf continued to gaze into her eyes and stroke her hair that cascaded wildly about her shoulders. They weren't eager to gather their clothes or join the others. The only thing that mattered was taking the time to treasure this blessed private moment.

She regarded how strikingly handsome he was sprawled across her body. His dark golden mane hung in loose curls around his sharply chiseled face. The corded muscles of his shoulders and arms bunched and flexed with every tender movement of his hands in her tangled hair. He was near godly as he pampered her in the afterglow of their lovemaking.

"What are you thinking about?" he asked.

Æsa breathed in deeply and smiled. "You. And how handsome you are. How handsome your son will be..."

Gustaf froze. The expression on his face was that of surprise and confusion.

Æsa looked him square in the eye. "I'm with child, m'lord."

****

Gustaf sat up and looked her up and down in her naked form. Her hair wildly fell in untidy cinnamon locks over large, full breasts but her stomach was flat with no sign of pregnancy. He almost allowed a smile to slip in, but then realized she couldn't possibly be with child. She was barren. She'd said so herself.

Why would she say differently now? Was she testing him to see if he truly meant what he said when he claimed he didn't need an heir? Thinking better of starting that argument, he retrieved her tunic from the ground and handed it to her. "Here. You'll catch your death of cold."

She yanked it from his hands and gasped. "Don't appease me with your idle concerns over my health. What should concern you is that I'm carrying your child."

"How is it that you're now pregnant as the sun sets—and rightly sure of it—yet just a few days ago, you feared you were incapable of such a thing? Can you explain that to me?"

"I was mistaken."

He groaned and gathered the rest of his belongings. "Mistaken, huh?" He almost laughed. He punched his arms through his sleeves of his tunic and secured his sword and scabbard at his hip. His boots were next, along with his wolf-skin cloak. "Delirious, more like it," he muttered under his breath.

"I heard that," she said disappointingly.

Gustaf heard her mumbling to herself as she dressed back into her clothes and leather shoes. When she swung the bear cloak around her shoulders, he spoke a little louder saying, "And to think Halldora insisted you'd be happy after I told you. Humph!"

"What did you say?"

Exasperated, Æsa squared her shoulders and gave him a stern look. "I said, Halldora insisted you'd be happy once I told you I was with child. I suppose she doesn't know everything!"

"Wait. Halldora told you that you were with child?"

She crossed her arms. "Aye. When you went off to hunt with the others, she came to me and told me I carried your son."

"A son."

"Aye, a son," Æsa reiterated. "Yours. Inside my womb."

Gustaf's voice rose. "Do you think Halldora speaks the truth?"

"Only you know her better than I. Would she lie about something like this?"

He released a breath he didn't know he held until now. "A son."

"Aye, Gustaf. A son."

He smiled. "My son."

Æsa stepped toward him and captured his hands, resting them on her belly. He stared at her stomach in awe.

Beneath his palms lay a tiny miracle, a blessing from the gods.

He collapsed to his knees and pressed his forehead to her navel. Tears of joy welled in his eyes as he came to accept the news.

Æsa threaded her fingers in his hair and cradled his head. "Can it be true?"

Gustaf lifted his face and peered into her loving eyes. "Halldora is an overbearing, intrusive old woman, but she is not a liar. Nor have I ever known her to be wrong. If she says a child grows in your womb, then 'tis so." He smiled as he heard his own words and leapt to his feet, embracing her in a joyous hug. "We're going to have a son. A strong, stubborn, unreasonable, mischievous son!"

"Only if he takes after you," she jested.

"Odin help us all if he does. Come, we must tell everyone the grand news!"

With an exuberant twist, he swung her up in his arms and carried her over to the tethered horse. Hoisting her up, he imagined bursting through the mead hall and proclaiming the condition of his betrothed to whole village. What a grand feast this would be, he thought.

As he dashed to the tree and jerked the knotted reins free, an arrow split the wind and sank deep into Gustaf's left shoulder.

Chapter Twenty-two

The piercing pain and momentous force of the projectile hurled Gustaf's upper body backward, forcing him to stagger on his feet. Everything happened so quickly: the horse reared, Æsa screamed, and both toppled to the ground in a heap as he suddenly realized they were under attack.

From a distance, Gustaf heard horses approaching, but his concern lay solely with his pregnant Æsa lying motionless on the ground after his horse scrambled to its feet and bolted. He shouted her name and stumbled to save her, only to be halted by another arrow penetrating his right thigh.

His leg gave out, and he fell to his knees, groaning in agony. He grasped the shaft of the wooden arrow sticking out of his leg and snapped off the end. By the time he did the same with the other in his shoulder, he saw five men galloping toward them, their swords unsheathed and ready to cut down anything in their path.

"Æsa!" he called, crawling toward her. He prayed to the gods that she was alive and reached out to touch her. Another arrow whizzed past his head, stopping him short.

He struggled to stand and unsheathed his weapon, limping several feet in front of his helpless Æsa to protect her. Planting his feet wide, he double fisted his sword and set his sights on the man in the lead. With one harrowing sweep, he slashed at the legs of the charging horse, causing the animal to plunge headfirst to the ground. The rider flipped over the animal's head, and his blade hurled from his hand.

Gustaf then dodged decapitation from an oncoming sword but couldn't get back into position quick enough to warrant a counterblow. Four mounted warriors surrounded him, trotting in a wide berth out of his reach. Outnumbered, he glanced between Æsa and his attackers, worrying whether she lay dead, or if she were alive, whether they'd make it out of this anyway.

Gustaf heard the man he'd knocked off his horse hobble across the ground to regain his sword, and staggered carefully to face him. He assumed the wounded man, whom he didn't recognize, was their leader, for no one spoke or struck out against him yet.

As the man on foot approached Æsa, the four circling him on horseback no longer held his attention. "Get away from her!" Gustaf ordered.

The man ignored him, sheathed his sword, and knelt on one knee beside Æsa. He stroked her cheek with the back of his hand and trailed his knuckles along the side of her neck to check for a pulse.

Gustaf's blood boiled as he was helpless to do

anything but watch this man touch her. The man sighed with relief, which temporarily gave Gustaf reprieve as well, until he glowered at his mounted archer.

"She lives, fortunately for you." The man's cold gray eyes then turned to Gustaf, and a sinister grin lifted one corner of his mouth. "As for you…you couldn't be less fortunate. The fact that you still breathe in my presence is a regrettable circumstance."

"Who are you?" Gustaf barked, adjusting his grip on his sword.

"I doubt you'd know my name, but Æsa here," he stated, gesturing toward her unconscious body, "knows me very well." He blatantly groped his crotch with his right hand as if to indicate the particular part of him with which she was acquainted.

Gustaf swallowed the bile that rose in his throat. His gut twisted and his body shook with fury. He caught a glimpse of a silver ring on the man's hand and recognition of the insignia on the ruby struck him like a slap in the face. "So, 'twas you who planted Ragnar's ring for Æsa to find on Skúvoy."

Gustaf turned over the events following their departure from the Faroes. He recalled the five men who followed them by boat, and the large sum of silver he paid to have them killed. Jørgen and Snorri had confirmed that five lay dead in the forest, but evidently it was not the correct group of men who'd met their fate.

The man's laughter interrupted Gustaf's tumbling

thoughts. "I can see you're quite confused. Allow me to enlighten you." He paced back and forth as he spoke. "You generously gave a group of six men a massive amount of silver to keep me from following you, but you failed to divvy it up among them. Your payment remained in one man's pocket and thus made it easier for me to offer him a more profitable deal. I proposed he keep it all to himself and walk away. I assume you're smart enough to fill in the rest." His conceited smile sliced through Gustaf. "Every man has a price," he continued. "And I'm willing to wager Æsa has one as well. Care to find out what that might be?"

"Touch her and you die," Gustaf warned, pointing his sword directly at the man's chest.

Again the man laughed, unshaken by the threat. "It bears mentioning that I know you're quite taken with the whore. So, this should be interesting." He waggled his brows in a taunting manner and lowered himself to his good knee, brushing her hair from her face.

Gustaf lunged forward, but the four on horseback halted his progress. He was incapable of moving without enduring some sort of injury from the three sword blades or the bow and arrow aimed at his heart. He searched for a way to escape their guard, but every scenario left him gravely wounded and powerless to save Æsa. He'd have to bide his time until a better opportunity presented itself. Either way, he'd not go down without a fight.

"Æsa, open your eyes," the man crooned. "I have a surprise for you." He shook her gently and, for a few moments, whispered words Gustaf could not hear.

Gustaf grew restless. He hated to think what this bastard would do once she came to. Silently, he prayed to his Almighty Odin that she'd not awaken and become a pawn. After that, he sent up a request to Thor that his mind be clear, his body strong, and his sword swift and accurate.

For once, he regretted stepping beyond the perimeter of the rune stones. If he'd remained within its boundaries, Halldora would have known he and Æsa were in danger, and she could alert his men. As it stood, the only chance he had of someone coming to his aid was if his riderless horse drew someone's attention.

"I grow impatient, Æsa." Distaste lathered the man's voice now. "Wake up." She didn't move an inch upon his command, and he gripped her cloak under her chin and lifted her head from the ground. "Wake up, you whore!"

His hand came down hard across her cheek, and Gustaf came undone. Adrenaline surged through his body, and Gustaf sprang forward, striking the muzzle of the horse in front of him. The animal reared and opened the tight circle, giving Gustaf a clear shot at the man who'd slapped Æsa. He was able to take a few steps forward before a sword blade struck him across the back. His thick wolf-skin cloak saved him from a debilitating wound, but the force propelled him facedown in the dirt.

Before he could get to his feet, he was jerked to his knees by his hair and held upright with a sword pointed at his back.

"Gustaf!"

Æsa's voice rang true and loud, a godsend to his ears, but when he turned his head in her direction, she was held captive with a dagger at her throat. He white-knuckled the grip of his sword, ready to thrust it behind him, but the tip of his enemy's blade pressed painfully into his spine.

"So, your name is Gustaf," the man said curiously. "Would that be Gustaf, the notorious eldest son of Rælik— the spawn of the man my father, Ragnar, killed so many years ago? I thought you were dead."

Gustaf reeled with shock. *Ragnar's son?* But Æsa said he was killed. Burned and beheaded, if he recalled. "I suppose I could say I heard the same about you, Asmundr."

"So, you *do* know me," Asmundr replied, looking down his nose at Æsa. "What else did this little bitch tell you about me?"

Gustaf bit his tongue over the name Asmundr called her and wished he were able to yank Asmundr's from his mouth. "Naught else of import, I assure you."

Asmundr's laughter cut through the dark forest like lightning, and Gustaf swore he'd personally cut out the man's voice box before he killed him slowly.

Asmundr rubbed his crooked nose along Æsa's soft throat. "I venture to say she probably forgot to mention that we were once lovers. That together we planned to go in search of my father's hidden silver. You know, the payment given for your father's murder. But Ragnar got jealous and banished me before I had a chance to whisk her away to safety. And then you came along and stole both my vengeance and my…" He regarded Æsa with lust and licked her behind the ear before saying, "my *thrall*."

"I'm not yours!" she screamed. "I never was!"

Asmundr tightened his arm around her waist and pushed the blade harder against her skin. "I didn't give you permission to speak, Æsa. Open your mouth again, and I'll cut out your tongue!" When she settled down, Asmundr praised her. "That's it. There's my obedient *thrall* I know and love." He then glared at Gustaf. "Before you even think of using that sword in one desperate attempt to save this woman, I suggest you drop it, lest I kill her right now."

"He lies, Gustaf," Æsa protested. "He'll not kill me. He needs me. I'm the only one who knows where the silver is buried. You know this. He cannot find the silver without my help, else he would've dug it up himself already."

Gustaf was torn. What Æsa said made perfect sense, but he wasn't so certain about Asmundr or how much he was willing to risk. He knew the man was ruthless and greedy, much like his father. But ultimately, it was her life at stake.

To his surprise, Asmundr released his hold on Æsa and sheathed his dagger. "What she says is true. I do need her. I cannot find the silver without her. Which means…" he said, drawing out his words on purpose, "I have no use for you." He locked gazes with the man standing behind Gustaf. "Kill him."

"Nay!" Æsa ran to Gustaf's aid, but Asmundr yanked

her back by the hair.

Gustaf spun wildly to his left and mowed the legs of his foe like a scythe. The man collapsed without rendering a single injury to Gustaf's back and screamed in pain at the stubs of bloodied flesh below his knees. Gustaf twirled his sword in his hands, tip downward, and thrust it deep into the suffering man's chest.

Jumping to his feet, Gustaf took on the next man who posed the most threat and snatched a dagger from his boot sheath. With precision and speed, he launched it in a sideways throw into the archer's shoulder and sent him off the back of his horse.

The next adversary tackled Gustaf from atop his horse and brought him to the ground. He grasped the broken arrow sticking out of Gustaf's shoulder and shoved it inward. Gustaf howled, dropping his sword and elbowing the man in the face. His opponent proved to have a savage doggedness equal to his own and didn't let go. Instead, the man wrapped his muscular arm around Gustaf's neck and applied pressure with a clinch he couldn't escape.

Struggling to breathe, Gustaf beat his fists on the man's head and tore at his eyes, anything to get him to release his chokehold. All his efforts failed, and gradually blackness seeped in around him. At the last second as he neared unconsciousness, Æsa's shriek sparked his eyes open. He couldn't die this way, nor could he allow Asmundr to inflict any more pain on her. He couldn't let Asmundr win. He willed himself to live.

Breathe! Fight!

"Please, Asmundr," Æsa pleaded. "I'll do whatever you want. I'll tell you where the silver is buried, but you must let Gustaf live. If you kill him, I'll take the secret to my grave. I swear it!"

The arm around Gustaf's neck dropped, and he crumpled to the ground, gasping for air. He coughed and choked, dragging a sliver of air into his dry, constricted throat, only to collapse in another fit of coughing. In the course of his struggle, he squinted through the blur to search for Æsa. He found her on her knees, begging at Asmundr's feet as he was grabbed by two men. With one on each arm, they hoisted him to his knees.

Asmundr sidestepped Æsa and approached Gustaf. "You know not when to quit, do you? You're begging for death. I can make it happen."

Æsa crawled toward him. "Please, Gustaf. Do what he says."

Gustaf tried to warn her to stay back, but his vocal cords had received too much damage to work. Asmundr backhanded her and continued to taunt him, despite Gustaf's attempt to rip free.

"Why do you risk so much for a whore?" Asmundr asked. "Why choose her over your own life? Better yet, I wonder who she'd choose if given a choice. Let's find out."

Gustaf thrashed and growled as he shook his head so Æsa would know he objected to whatever Asmundr asked her to do. He ground his teeth, hoping she'd just leave him behind and run for her life. He willed her to flee, implored it with every ounce of his being, but she came to her feet as Asmundr bid her.

He crossed his arms. "You want Gustaf to live?"

Frantically, she nodded as tears spilled from her eyes.

"Then proclaim your love for me, and he'll not die by my hand. Kiss me...like you mean it...and I won't kill him."

Gustaf knew Asmundr would kill him no matter what she did, but he couldn't bear the sight of her kissing him. He closed his eyes.

Asmundr turned and saw Gustaf's attempt to avoid bearing witness to Æsa's choice. He drew his dagger, pressing it against Gustaf's throat. "Open your eyes! You'll watch this, or I'll kill you now!"

"Nay, Asmundr!" Æsa cried. "Please. I'll do as you ask."

With the blade at Gustaf's neck, he gestured Æsa forward with his free hand. "Say what I want to hear."

Æsa squeezed her eyes shut as if to practice her words in her own mind first. "I love you, Asmundr."

"Now, show me," Asmundr demanded. "And if I so much as feel one hint of insincerity from your lips, I shall gut your Gustaf like a fish." She hesitated for a second longer than Asmundr was willing to tolerate. "Choose, Æsa! Me—or him! Make your choice!"

Æsa stepped into Asmundr's arms, tentative and slow. She placed her hands upon his chest and stared into the eyes of his most hated enemy. Inside, he screamed as he watched Æsa embrace and kiss him. And he vomited in his throat when they shared tongues like long-lost lovers.

The knife at his neck slipped away, and Gustaf hung his head in defeat. Æsa had played the part and sacrificed her dignity to spare his life. Or so she was meant to believe. Gustaf knew better. No matter what she said or did, Asmundr would have him killed.

"You chose well, Æsa. Now, where is the silver?"

"Ragnar said he buried it in the land where you were born."

Asmundr contemplated her answer. "Tromsø... He buried it in Tromsø. All these years..." His eyes suddenly glinted with urgency. "We haven't much time. Soon the sun will cease to rise where we're going, and I'll be damned if the polar night will keep me from finding Ragnar's plunder." He shoved Æsa forward. "Quickly. Mount up."

Æsa dragged her feet, refusing to leave Gustaf behind, but Asmundr enforced his authority by throwing her up onto the horse himself.

Gustaf stared at her, knowing she believed Asmundr's promise. And because he didn't want her to witness his death, he'd let her believe it. He looked at her reassuringly and mouthed the words, *'Tis all right. Go. I will find you.*

Tears filled her eyes as she continued to gaze at him in his subservient position. His heart split in two as he watched her die inside for the decision she had no choice but to make. He'd not hold it against her. He knew who she truly loved.

Love had bound them together in a way no man could sever—not even Asmundr, who'd secretly handed his dagger to one of the men at Gustaf's right.

Asmundr mounted behind Æsa with a casual, arrogant air and snuggled up close to her. "We shall wait for you north of Lillehammer," he said to his trio of men.

Gustaf watched Asmundr trot away. All the fight and vigor that once filled his heart was now gone. He looked down at his wounds. Dark crimson patches stained his breeches and tunic where the broken shafts of two arrows protruded. His strength drained as he bled.

The man chosen for the deed approached Gustaf and stood like a towering wall of stone before him. Gustaf closed his eyes and braced himself for the dagger that would plunge between his ribs.

Chapter Twenty-three

Øyven gazed over the crowd of villagers in the mead hall as he sat on an outlying bench away from the noise, the dancing, and the joyous commotion. He was in no mood to join in, for his chieftain had yet to return from his ride with Æsa. Gustaf had promised he'd not miss the feast, and it wasn't like him to break an oath. His absence was clearly out of the norm but went unnoticed by the celebrating villagers who ate and drank in gluttonous proportions.

No longer able to endure his climbing concern, Øyven made his way toward Halldora resting comfortably by the fire in the center of the hall. If anyone knew Gustaf's whereabouts, she would.

Wise silver eyes locked on him before he sat beside her. He regarded her carefully. "You know what brings me to you."

"Aye," Halldora said plainly. "But I cannot help you. Gustaf has either found a way to keep his mind empty, or he's traveled beyond the perimeter of the stones."

"You cannot hear anything?" Øyven implored.

"Naught pertaining to Gustaf." She laid her hand upon his and gave a squeeze. "But worry not. Æsa has marvelous news to share with him, so I suspect they're..." She paused, then said, "rejoicing in secret, if you will. I'm certain he'll return soon."

The old woman's words did little to soothe him. He wasn't usually one to assume the worst, like Snorri, but he couldn't help think that Gustaf might be in trouble.

"The only trouble Gustaf finds," Halldora answered for him, "is avoiding temptation where his dearest Æsa is concerned. If I were you, I'd respect his wish for privacy as he's gone to great lengths to keep us out of his affairs."

Øyven accepted Halldora's advice but wasn't completely satisfied. If anything, he needed to remove himself from the heat of the congested mead hall and clear his head. Nodding his thanks, he left and stepped out into the cool night air.

Rows of empty longhouses lined each side of the mead hall while a group of servants continued to roast the remainder of the bear on a spit. Even they were oblivious to the fact that the very man who'd killed the animal was not around to commemorate the successful hunt.

Again, he tried to extinguish his pessimistic thoughts and ventured toward the stables. Caring for animals often left him with a sense of solace, as they weren't loud and obnoxious like some people he knew. They never complained about the rigors of daily life, and they held their emotions in check for even the slightest attention from a kind human.

Entering the stable, he stopped short to find Helga,

and she gasped. "Forgive me," Øyven apologized. "I didn't know you were in here."

Helga went back to petting his horse in the stall. "I hope you don't mind, but I fed and watered your horse as I was told you didn't want him turned out with the others to graze."

Øyven approached her, but the thought of Halldora slipped into his thoughts, and he kept his distance. "Are there no boys for this sort of labor?"

Her chin fell. "Aye, there are, but I enjoy helping."

Øyven noticed her shivering and immediately removed his cloak from his shoulders and draped it around hers.

"Thank you," she said softly.

Her kind eyes met his, and he forgot all about Halldora. Before he realized, he reached up and touched the bashful girl's cheek. "You're so beautiful."

Upon his compliment, she stepped back from his touch, reminding him of his mistake. A dark stable was not exactly the most appropriate place for words of endearment. "Would you like to join me in the mead hall?" Øyven asked, gesturing outside the barn.

"I would like that very much."

"I expect your grandmother would prefer that as well."

Helga giggled ever so quietly and took the arm he offered her. He had to admit he loved her timid laughter, and he also understood why Halldora was so protective of the girl. She was pleasing to the eye with hair like spun silk, as golden as the blazing sun. Her eyes were like sapphires, polished and sparkling. Her lips were full and alluring, her nose small and straight. If he didn't know better, he would have thought her to be the daughter of the goddess Freyja.

"Why did you leave the feast to come to the stables?" Helga finally asked, interrupting his thoughts.

Øyven cleared his head and recalled his missing chieftain. "Gustaf and Æsa have not returned. I'm worried about them as he assured me he would—" From his peripheral vision, he caught sight of a riderless horse careening in from the forest. It trotted several yards in front of them through the settlement and halted in the field where the other horses grazed.

He and Helga raced toward the animal and verified it was indeed Gustaf's steed once they were closer. He soothed the agitated horse with a calming voice before snagging the reins and inspected it for signs of injury. The only thing the horse suffered was mild exhaustion.

Øyven's greatest fear was confirmed. Something was definitely amiss, as Gustaf would never forget to tether his horse. But what caused the animal to spook and run away without him?

He turned to Helga and mounted Gustaf's horse without hesitation. "I need you to fetch Jørgen and Snorri from the mead hall. Tell them Gustaf is in danger."

He then made a mad dash in the direction from where the horse had come. He tore through the forest, knowing he had to go beyond the perimeter of the rune stones to find Gustaf and Æsa. Galloping along, he called for them, while more dread filled his heart the longer he traveled without their reply.

He ran for what seemed like an eternity until the boundary of the flat, carved stones shone under the moonlit sky. He urged the horse onward, hurdling over them so as not to disrupt the spell. As soon as its hooves touched ground, he pulled back on the reins and the animal skidded to a sliding halt. A gruesome sight tainted the forest floor and Øyven couldn't believe his eyes.

A horse with a gaping wound across its chest lay dead and steaming, and a man he didn't recognize lay sprawled and hacked in two, his legs horrifically severed from his body. The coppery smell of blood saturated the eerie scene before him.

"Gustaf!" he yelled, but only his own voice echoed back at him. "Æsa! Where are you?"

Searching beyond the carnage, Øyven saw another body, facedown, unmoving. His entire body recoiled when he recognized the thick gray wolf-skin cloak on the man's back, unwilling to believe it was his chieftain and friend lying dead amongst the others.

Reluctantly, Øyven dismounted and stared at the crumpled form. His stomach rolled, sickened by the possibility that he'd found Gustaf moments too late. He stepped forward, his feet heavy. A sour taste poisoned his tongue. *Am I too late?*

He'd never forgive himself if he was. He should've listened to his gut and gone searching for Gustaf long before now. Perhaps he could've prevented this, or at least come to his aid. When he stood over the man, he closed his eyes as he knelt, mentally preparing himself for the worst.

He carefully rolled the body over, and Gustaf's pale face gleamed amid the shadows of the forest. His chieftain's eyes shot open at the same time he gasped for air.

"Gustaf!" Øyven exclaimed, stunned. "You're alive!" His hands shook as he cradled his chieftain in his lap and scanned the wounds, the blood, and the broken arrows that protruded from Gustaf's body. "Who did this? Where is Æsa?"

Æsa's name resounded on Gustaf's lips in a listless whisper.

"Aye, Æsa," Øyven encouraged. "Where is she?"

Gustaf closed his eyes and swallowed, trying desperately to answer. "Taken. Asmundr."

"Asmundr?" Øyven's mind reeled as he remembered the name. "But I thought Æsa said he was dead."

Gustaf slowly shook his head. "Alive." He tried to say more, but the struggle to speak was too much for him.

"Shh…say no more. We'll find her." Øyven tried to gather Gustaf in his arms and lift him to his feet, but the burly warrior, weakened by loss of blood, proved too heavy.

"Leave me. Find Æsa," Gustaf commanded.

"I have to get you on the horse!"

Gustaf groaned, trying to find the strength to move,

but his wounds pained him far too much. He collapsed in exhaustion, and fell unconscious again.

Øyven yelled at the top of lungs, frustrated that he couldn't physically get his chieftain off the ground. Panic overwhelmed him as he realized Gustaf was slowly dying in his arms. "Stay with me, Gustaf! Stay with me!" He shouted for help in a last desperate attempt and suddenly heard hoofbeats approaching.

Øyven's stomach leapt into his throat. He was useless to defend his vulnerable chieftain without a weapon and terrified Gustaf's attackers had come back to finish the job. But then he heard Jørgen's frantic voice and breathed a sigh of relief. "Over here! Gustaf is dying! Hurry!"

Snorri and Jørgen burst from the darkness and vaulted from their steeds with lightning speed, sliding to their knees at Gustaf's side. They were full of panic, dismay, and questions that Øyven couldn't answer.

Without a word, Snorri grabbed Gustaf's arm and jerked his chieftain's body forward, hauling him over his shoulder. He carried him to his horse and threw him across the front of the saddle. Mounting behind him, he spun his horse around and sprinted off.

Jørgen exchanged a helpless look with Øyven. "Who did this?"

"Gustaf said it was Asmundr."

"Ragnar's son?"

"Aye, and he took Æsa."

"Why?"

"I didn't get to ask. Gustaf..." Øyven hung his head, feeling as if his whole world was caving in around him. After he'd lost his whole family to Fairhair's expanding reign, Gustaf had become not only a father figure, but a dear friend. He'd taken him in and given him a purpose in life, something no one else had cared to provide.

As Øyven stared in sorrow, a white scrap of cloth blew across the ground. Though it was tattered and stained with blood, he noticed the colorful embroidered stitches dotting the fabric. He picked it up and gazed at Jørgen. Both were filled with dread as they realized it was Æsa's gift to Gustaf, the one he always had tucked in his sleeve.

And she was nowhere to be found.

Chapter Twenty-four

Halldora ripped open Gustaf's kirtle and assessed his wounds as Helga and Gustaf's loyal men stood helplessly around her. A blazing fire crackled in the old woman's hearth, and herbs of every kind hung within reach in the rafters above their heads. Vials of various liquids, pastes, and poultices lined a shelf on the back wall, and strange animal skulls stared at them from the thatched ceiling.

Standing in Halldora's home was enough to make any man feel uneasy, but the ghastly sight of Gustaf pierced with arrows and stabbed below his ribs was more unnerving than all the oddities contained there.

Øyven cringed as Halldora carefully inserted her bony fingers inside Gustaf's knife wound and felt around to make sure no vessels had been severed or any vital organs damaged. When she retracted her fingers, she said nothing, but a look of relief eased across her brow. At least one thing fell in his chieftain's favor.

"We should have ridden closer to the five dead in the forest instead of just counting them," Snorri muttered bitterly. "We would've known we were still being followed."

"I did as I was told," Jørgen said.

"You failed him," Snorri accused, pointing at him. "You failed to protect the man who always protected you. I told you we should've looked at their faces. You wouldn't listen to me. And now, our chieftain fights for his life because of your mistake."

"Enough!" Halldora bellowed. "You do Gustaf no good blaming each other. He hears you, and yet he blames only himself. He grows weaker as he holds on to his regret. I need him to be strong, and I need you to hold your tongue, Snorri."

"What can we do, Halldora?" Jørgen asked, his voice straining with guilt.

Halldora ignored Jørgen's question and placed her hands on Gustaf's bare chest. She closed her eyes and listened. Her wrinkled face puckered even more at the picture she saw through his thoughts. "He is filled with rage. His heart beats in wild succession as this Asmundr fellow hits Æsa. She is begging at Asmundr's feet, but he does not care. He taunts Gustaf. He forces Æsa to make a choice. She stands proud and comes into Asmundr's arms." Halldora gasps. "She kisses him."

"That bitch!" Snorri snarled. "She played us."

Øyven took offense to Snorri's allegation. "Æsa would not do that."

"Then why did she betray Gustaf in such a way?"

"I know not. Perhaps she felt she could distract Asmundr long enough—"

"You're blind and naïve, Øyven," Snorri interrupted. "I always knew she had an evil side, but you all refused to admit it because Gustaf was smitten with her."

"She loves him," Øyven insisted. "She wouldn't do this."

"She is a whore. Whores know not what love is."

Halldora's eyes flashed open. "One more outburst, and I'll throw you both out myself."

Snorri quickly clamped his mouth shut, but Øyven was not so obedient. "Æsa loved him, Halldora. You know this as well as I. Ask Gustaf why she kissed Asmundr."

The old woman closed her eyes again and tried to hear Gustaf's thoughts, while everyone else was held in suspense. Her fragile hands trembled upon his chest and her white brow furrowed over a troubled face. "She kisses him to make him believe she loves him. She promises to help him find the hoard of silver he desires, if he promises to let Gustaf live." She listened intently as if his thoughts had become more difficult to hear, until suddenly she yanked her hands away. Gasping, she shook her hands as if they'd been burned and looked fearfully into Øyven's eyes. "Asmundr did not uphold his end of the bargain, and Gustaf knew his fate before 'twas sealed with that kiss. If Gustaf lives through this, there will be no stopping him in his vengeance. I've never felt this kind of fury from one man. Not even in a *berserker*. If any of you value your lives, you'll not stand in his way."

Øyven came to her on bended knee. "He must live,

Halldora. Vengeance or not, he must live. Please."

Her tired gray eyes searched over the seven warriors in the room. "I'll need four strong men to hold Gustaf down. I need to extract the arrows and cauterize the wounds if he's to have any chance to live."

Helga touched Halldora's arm. "Let me, Grandmother. My hands are smaller and steadier than yours. I'll remove the arrows if you tell me how."

"Can you stomach it, child?"

Helga didn't hesitate in her reply.

"And I'll be one of the strong four," Øyven volunteered readily.

Halldora cocked her head with pity. "My dear Øyven, I know you mean well. 'Tis not the strength of your body I need, but the strength of your mind. Gustaf will howl in pain all through the night as we do this. Your heart cannot take it. His screams will haunt you, I know this."

"I will block it out," he argued.

"You want to help your chieftain?" Halldora asked. "Then take Ketill and Ulfr with you and search for Æsa. Find her and bring her back safely."

Øyven nodded once with determination and leapt to his feet. He'd do this for Gustaf because he knew Gustaf would do it for him. As he marched past the hearth, he locked eyes with Snorri. The two men scowled at each other, holding each other's glare. For once, Øyven wouldn't be the first to look away. He stood his ground until Snorri yielded.

As he reached for the door and pulled it open, Snorri seized his forearm. "You're going to need this," he said, gifting him with his own leather belt that held his sheathed sword.

Øyven was surprised. Snorri wasn't the kind of man to admit when he was wrong, or apologize when he was out of line. He was a warrior who reacted solely on instinct and barreled through with muscle might, leaving no room for second guesses or petty pardons. Knowing this was Snorri's way of extending a peace offering, he accepted the weapon and hurried out the door.

****

Halldora was right. Gustaf's continual cries of pain had plagued his mind as he and Jørgen's sons saddled up and rode long into the wee hours of the night searching for Æsa. His unbearable screams echoed in his head the entire time they'd made a sweeping pass of the surrounding area. Traveling as far as several kilometers north of Lake Mjøsa didn't ease his torment either. As Halldora predicted, he was haunted by the thought of Gustaf's agony, and there was no way to make it stop.

Though Øyven grew weary, he doubled back, returning to the scene of the attack. The only thing he recovered was Gustaf's bloody sword lying near the place where he'd fallen. By sunup, their pursuit had come to a disappointing end, and the three men barely had enough strength to keep their eyes open.

After they cared for their spent horses, Øyven dragged his fatigued, sorrowful body to the door of Halldora's hut, Gustaf's sword in hand. Gazing at the intricately decorated weapon of rubies and silver filigree that had once belonged to Gustaf's father, he couldn't bring himself to enter. He hadn't come back empty-handed, but he'd failed to recover what he knew Gustaf treasured most.

He imagined the pain Gustaf had endured under Halldora's care would be nothing compared to waking and finding Æsa gone without a trace. With the weight of that burden resting on Øyven's shoulders, he slid down Halldora's door until his bottom hit the ground. His eyes automatically closed as he rested his weary head on his knee, and for one short moment, sleep overcame him.

****

Øyven fell backward as Halldora's door was pulled open. The sword he'd been reverently holding fell from his grasp and thumped against the wooden threshold. He shook the sleepiness from his head and blinked repeatedly, seeing Gustaf's men exit in slow single file. Each sorrowful man looked as if he'd aged ten years.

Øyven gathered Gustaf's sword and jumped to his feet. "How does he fare?"

Snorri kept walking. "He sleeps. Halldora gave him a potion to help him rest."

"Will he be all right?"

"Only time will tell."

This was not the news Øyven wanted to hear, but it was better than he'd feared given the grief-stricken appearance of the six depleted warriors staggering out.

Looking back toward Halldora's door where his chieftain lay on the other side, he was compelled to enter. Teeth clenched, heart constricted, he took a deep breath and pushed inside.

The scene took his breath away. Blood-soaked cloths lay in a heap on the rush-covered floor. Basins of bloody water sat on every flat surface. Golden flames danced in a warm crackling fire in the hearth, but every soul in the room lay quiet and still, eyes closed.

Halldora slept slumped in a rickety chair. Wisps of thinning white hair fell over her ashen face, which told of her great efforts this night. Helga lay in the boxbed to the right, her appearance just as disheveled as her grandmother's. To the left lay Gustaf on his back, his freshly sewn wounds resembling a tapestry of embroidery stitches, yet more crude in nature. His body had been divested of clothing, which now lay soiled at his feet on the boxbed. Draped across his waist was a thick animal hide, and his bare feet stuck out at the end.

Gustaf looked like a corpse as he lay half-naked upon the narrow bed. He appeared a conquered warrior who'd fought his last battle and would never rise to lift his sword again.

"I know 'tis difficult for you to look upon this man." Halldora's voice broke through the silence. "A man you've always respected and revered, and see him in such a vulnerable state."

Øyven said nothing but knew she'd heard his mournful thoughts. He neared his chieftain and laid the prized weapon at his side. He hoped the sword would one day find its way back into Gustaf's grasp, where it could be wielded to help right the wrong and bring swift justice to his foes. He couldn't bear the thought of the blade being ceremoniously buried with him, never to be brandished again.

"You need to prepare yourself, Øyven. He's lost a great deal of blood, and his fever is setting in. He'll grow delirious in the next hours, and 'twill be more difficult to sustain him if he refuses food and water. I'll continue to care for him, but there is only so much I can do. There may come a time when his body gives up."

Øyven squeezed his eyes shut in an effort to restrain his emotions. He clenched his jaw to stop the trembling of his lower lip and blinked away the sting of hot tears. "There are some things you do not know, Halldora." He turned to face her and leveled his gaze onto hers, undeterred by the old woman's sympathetic stare. "If anyone can pull through this, 'tis Gustaf. He will live." He drew himself up to his full height and said again, "He *will* live."

****

Æsa sat in solitude in Lillehammer's majestic foothills overlooking the Lågen River surrounded by mountains. The blissful view of the dawn breaking over the horizon did little to ease her tormented mind.

Did Gustaf understand that she'd had no choice but to leave him behind to guide Asmundr to the buried silver he so greedily treasured? And would he forgive her for betraying him? She hoped that he would, as she'd only done those things to spare the life of her unborn son's father.

She recalled how shameful she'd felt, kissing Asmundr in such an intimate manner in front of Gustaf. The grotesque thickness and taste of his stale tongue and lips had turned her stomach short of vomiting. It sickened her even now. But all she had to do was keep her end of the bargain and all would be better. How she'd escape Asmundr and get back to Gustaf was another matter entirely.

She thought about how she might have to kill Asmundr in order to get away. Though she'd gladly plunge a dagger into his cold, merciless heart, she hoped Gustaf would come to save her and bring an unrestrained wrath with him.

"On your feet, Æsa," Asmundr commanded from behind her. "Grimr and the men approach, and we need to move onward."

Æsa purposefully ignored him. It might bring her nothing but pain, but she didn't care. She wouldn't give him the satisfaction of thinking he could command her as he saw fit. He'd not broken her yet.

She heard her name on his lips again and pretended not to hear.

"I said," Asmundr growled, snagging a fistful of hair and tugging her upright. "On. Your. Feet!"

Æsa refused to scream. Instead, she laughed at him.

"What is so amusing, *thrall?*"

"Gustaf will kill you," she said with a sneer. "He'll hunt you down and kill you with a vengeance you've yet to see possible from one man. I almost pity you."

It was Asmundr's turn to laugh. "Do not pity me. 'Twould be a waste of your energy. A corpse doesn't have the luxury of vengeance." A cruel spark of delight flashed in his heartless eyes before he tightened his fist in her hair and dragged her toward his horse.

"What are you saying?" Æsa asked, grasping at his hand.

He shoved her against the horse's flank and ripped her arm behind her back, crushing her into the animal's body until she submitted to the awkward bend of her elbow. His mouth accosted her ear. "A dead man can do naught to save you. The only benefit he leaves behind is the food his rotting corpse will bring to the worms of the ground. Unless, of course, his men choose to give him a king's funeral, where he'd then be food for the fishes."

Æsa froze at the grim meaning behind Asmundr's vulgar words. "Gustaf is dead? You killed him?"

Asmundr released her. "Not I, for I gave you my word I wouldn't. Grimr, on the other hand, doesn't bargain with whores. I think 'tis because his mother was a whore," he said, pretending to ponder Grimr's mad behavior.

Æsa flung herself at Asmundr and tried to gouge out his eyes, but he was prepared for her reaction and caught her wrists. He held her claws at bay and laughed at her.

"I hate you!" she spat.

"I know, love. But you'll learn to tolerate me. Fortunately for you, we race against time, and my desire to find my father's buried silver outweighs my desire to bend you over and slake my urges."

"You've made the gravest of mistakes, Asmundr, for I'll not lead you anywhere! I'll take the location of your father's silver to my grave, this I swear!" Æsa shrieked with tears streaming from her eyes. "You'll have to torture me, and even then, 'twill not escape my lips!"

"That's where you're wrong, my dear." Asmundr clenched his fist and swung a punch that sent her crashing to the ground at his feet. Grimr and the men rode up just in time to see Asmundr shaking his smarting hand.

"You waited until now to tell her?" Grimr asked, putting two and two together.

"I couldn't be certain of his demise until you returned. For all I knew, Gustaf could've killed you after I left."

"I'm glad to know you maintain such confidence in me."

Asmundr grinned at Grimr's sarcasm and shook his

head as he regarded the foolish woman at his feet. "Help me get her on the horse. We've a long journey ahead of us."

"Every jaunt with you is long, m'lord," Grimr said dismounting.

Asmundr watched as Grimr bent and hoisted Æsa over his shoulder with ease. "Aye, but at least we'll travel in peace now. Just be thankful of that." He shook his hand once more as the ache began to settle in.

Chapter Twenty-five

One month later

Øyven opened his sluggish eyes to the glaring morning sun and stretched his aching back caused by the cramped position he'd slept in on the stoop in front of Halldora's hut. Like so many nights, he'd kept a vigil at the door, eager for the day when Gustaf would open his eyes and speak sensibly.

For days, Gustaf had suffered through a debilitating fever that drenched his body in sweat and convulsed his muscles with chills. If he wasn't fighting that, he was talking out of his head. Though Halldora had made every effort to keep nourishment in his body, he'd often grown combatant, struggling against anyone who aimed to touch him.

If anything had proved to be a good sign, it was Gustaf's readiness to engage in a brawl. Halldora had been able to get food and water in his system on a regular basis, but it never went without a struggle. Eventually, the fever had subsided, and with it, the delirium. Gustaf had then fallen into a deep sleep. The fight to live in Gustaf had slowly dissipated and, in the last few weeks, the warrior hadn't moved a muscle.

Everyone in the settlement had prayed for their fallen hero, that soon he'd wake from his nightmare. But every day brought Øyven disappointment, and it would seem this dawn was no different.

As he stood to regain the life in his legs, he was struck by the distant sound of hammering. Curiosity overtook him and he padded in the direction of the lakeshore. Upon seeing the men of the village working in collective harmony, he rubbed his eyes. Some straddled logs, ripping bark and hand-hewing the timber. Others cut the wood into planks, while most were constructing what looked like the beginnings of a hull for a longship.

Øyven made his way down to the meadow to inquire about the sudden fuss over a ship. He found Jørgen directing the construction. "Where are we headed? I wasn't told we were going on a journey."

Jørgen regarded him with hesitation. "'Tis not for us that we build the vessel. 'Tis for Gustaf's journey to Valhalla."

Øyven felt his heart stop. He looked back toward Halldora's hut then glared at Jørgen. "Has he…" He could not bring himself to ask.

Jørgen clasped his shoulder. "Soon, Øyven. 'Twill be soon."

He shoved Jørgen's hand away. "You're wrong!"

The hammering and sawing of wood slowly ceased and

every eye turned to stare. It was obvious to Øyven that everyone had worried he'd react this way and purposely kept the task of building Gustaf's funeral ship from him.

Snorri laid down his tools and approached. "Øyven, 'tis time to let go. Many weeks have come and gone. With each day, his heart beats slower."

"Nay."

"Gustaf is giving up—"

"Nay. *You're* giving up!" Øyven shouted. "You're *all* giving up! If Gustaf knew you were doing this, he'd not stand for it."

Jørgen tried again to reason with Øyven, but Øyven circumvented his attempts. Overcome with anger and resentment, he tore from the shoreline and ran as fast as he could to where Gustaf slept. Unconcerned by the ruckus he made as he burst through the old woman's door, he locked eyes on Halldora, who was standing over the bedside performing a sacred ritual with incense and lifted prayers to Odin. She chanted as she swayed:

"Rouse your chosen champion… Bid him to rise up and enter into your Valhalla.

Bid the Valkyries to proffer wine, for a prince is about to come."

Øyven knocked the bowl of incense from her grasp and gripped both her arms, pulling her away from Gustaf's body. "Stop this. Do not beckon the gods to take him." He pointed at his chieftain's motionless body. "He still breathes. His heart still beats. He's not yet gone from this world, and yet you summon Odin to carry him off. Why?"

Halldora looked into his eyes, her voice barely a whisper. "I hear nothing from Gustaf. His spirit is gone. Only a body remains."

"What do you mean you hear nothing? Surely he hasn't forgotten about what Asmundr has done to him. That Æsa still remains in his clutches unless he rescues her. She needs him!"

Halldora shook her head. "There is naught. No rage. No Æsa."

"Remind him!" Øyven roared. "You said yourself he can hear us."

"I've tried to talk to him, but he doesn't listen to what I say."

"He does not need to hear your mindless drivel, woman. He needs to get angry! He needs to know his Æsa's life is at stake should he do naught but die a *straw death*!"

Spurred into desperation, Øyven rushed to Gustaf's bedside and slapped him across the face. "Get up! Open your eyes and live!" He bent and vigorously shook his chieftain. "Find your will to live, my lord!"

When Gustaf didn't so much as move, Øyven took out Æsa's embroidered cloth he'd kept on his person and shoved it into Gustaf's lax palm. "Feel it," he demanded, squeezing the warrior's fingers around it. "Grasp it and prove you can hear me. Come on, Gustaf! I know you can hear me!"

Gustaf's fist contracted around the fabric, and Halldora gasped. "Keep at it, Øyven. 'Tis working. He hears you!"

Øyven glanced down at the fist holding tight to the material and he continued. "Aye, Gustaf. Get mad. Get very mad."

"Hit him again," Halldora instructed with a smile.

Reluctantly, Øyven threw his fist down hard upon Gustaf's chest. "Fight! Live!"

Halldora gasped again, her eyes wide with hope. "Asmundr's face flashed before Gustaf's eyes. He relives the day. He sees Æsa crying."

Øyven pressed his open palm on the blazing scar on Gustaf's left shoulder. Gustaf flinched but did not budge to prevent the assault on his injured body. Øyven didn't let up. He put all his weight on the wound and growled as he tortured his chieftain. "Feel that? Feel what Asmundr has done to you? What do you think he'll do to Æsa? Are you going to let it happen? Are you going to let him—"

Gustaf's free hand thrust like a crushing vise under Øyven's chin, squeezing his throat, choking him. His eyes, alight with fire and fury, bore into Øyven's as if he were the enemy. As if he were Asmundr himself.

Struggling to breathe, Øyven grasped at the surprisingly strong hand around his throat, trying to break free. "Gusta—"

Halldora cackled behind him, giving no aid to his predicament.

"A—little—help," Øyven choked out.

Snorri burst through the door in time to see a

disoriented Gustaf about to strangle Øyven. "My lord! Release him!" Snorri grasped his chieftain's hand and pried it free from Øyven's neck.

Gasping for air, Øyven dropped to the floor, his throat burning and his head pounding. The commotion continued between Snorri and Gustaf on the boxbed above him, while Øyven labored to draw air into his starved lungs. Halldora resumed laughing in the background, and Snorri shouted in exasperation for Jørgen, despite the fact that Gustaf still fought like a demon.

Hearing all the mayhem, Jørgen finally entered and helped secure Gustaf's arms. With an able-bodied man on each side, they held him down and tried to gain his attention.

"Gustaf! My lord! 'Tis I, Jørgen! Settle yourself and look at me. We wish no harm to you. Stop your thrashing."

Gustaf slowly recognized his own men and looked back and forth between the two, finding his bearings.

Winded but relieved, Øyven gathered himself off the floor and stood to face his chieftain. Gustaf lay pinned on the boxbed, his breathing just as labored as that of the two giants who held him captive. His ferocity had been subdued for the moment, but Øyven knew the full potential of Gustaf's wrath was yet to be unleashed.

"Good to have you back, m'lord," Øyven greeted, rubbing his tender throat.

Snorri and Jørgen released their hold on his arms and helped Gustaf sit upright. Gustaf examined the three scars marring his body and clearly remembered the men who'd ambushed him. "If my brother Dægan was still alive to herald this moment, I know he'd have something poetically moving to say. But what I lack in speech, I make up for in determination. Let my actions speak for themselves, for I will have my vengeance. As the last living son of Rælik, I will defend my father's honor and uphold his noble name. Rally the men for council." He clenched the embroidered cloth that lay in his palm. "My Æsa needs me."

****

Æsa resorted to riding in silence on the back of one of Asmundr's men's horse—anything to keep from having to ride with Asmundr. Since she'd come to, she'd refused to be near him, threatening to walk alongside the horses, if necessary. But given Asmundr's desire to beat the polar night that would soon cloak his homeland of Tromsø in complete darkness, he allowed her this one request.

They had journeyed for weeks through the harsh landscape, stopping only for necessity. Asmundr proved to be a fanatic the closer they got to Norway's arctic frontier. Not even the increased snowfall slowed his pursuit.

If it hadn't been for the fact that she carried Gustaf's child, Æsa would have leaped from one of the many cliff edges to the frigid water below. She would have welcomed death in any form rather than stay one more day as Asmundr's prisoner.

As it was, she had much to lose if she gave in to a voluntary death. The child that grew inside her was a miraculous gift, and she'd do all she could to see it born healthy and strong. She owed that much to Gustaf.

At times, she was moved to tears thinking of him and how he died to save her. Often she'd weep in uncontrollable sobs, but it had driven Asmundr to anger, which earned her many beatings. Now, her sorrow had turned to stark bitterness. Her tears had dried up, and all that was left was a shimmer of hope in the form of an unborn child, the spark that kept her going. She promised herself she would prevail and that their son would live to carry on his father's noble name.

More importantly, she had to make certain Asmundr never found out about her condition. She knew if he came into such knowledge, he'd use it against her.

As they crested the final ridge of their voyage, the beautiful valley of Tromsø emerged before them, surrounded by a channel of cobalt-blue water and a sharp range of snow-covered mountains to the north. The location was a virtual fortress, a breathtaking sight. Æsa could hardly believe that one so ugly and evil as Asmundr could be born in a place so beautiful.

He sat in reminiscence on his horse, admiring the splendor of his birthplace for reasons Æsa assumed differed from hers. He stretched out his arm and gestured over the entire area as if it all belonged to him. "There 'tis. My homeland. And somewhere amid this great land, where few men have had the courage to venture, lies my father's hoard of silver—soon to be mine." He reined his horse around and rode up to Æsa, regarding her coldly. "Where do we proceed from here?"

She didn't know the exact place Ragnar had buried the blood money, for she only overheard details describing it— particulars that made little sense to someone who was unfamiliar with Ragnar's sordid past.

"Answer me, Æsa!" Asmundr growled, jerking hard on the bit in his horse's mouth.

Æsa flinched, then trembled with fear.

"M'lord," one man finally said. "The woman shivers with cold. I can feel it against my back. We're all cold and exhausted. Might we settle in for the night and resume our quest at first light?"

Asmundr rolled his eyes. "I suppose we can wait until morn. Judging by the sun's position on the horizon, we have but a month before the season of Mørketid is upon us." He looked at Æsa, his steel-gray eyes flaring with revulsion. "Pray we find the silver before the polar night. If I do not have it in my possession before then, you'll pay dearly for it."

Chapter Twenty-six

The mead hall was again crowded with men. This time the atmosphere of the gathering reeked of tension and rising aggravation.

Gustaf sat at the head of the long table, Jørgen and Snorri to his left and Øyven to his immediate right. Down the length of the table, the rest of his loyal men and their kinsmen filled the benches with a heated discussion.

Gustaf listened as each man argued the best course of action for finding and saving Æsa. Several suggested they should solicit the help of the neighboring clans, which many disputed as time-consuming and unnecessary since there were now only four men keeping her captive. Others suggested exploiting Halldora and her magical powers in hopes she'd cast a crippling spell of blinding headaches followed by vertigo. Though facetious in nature, a raging case of watery bowels had also been proposed.

After listening to countless ideas, Gustaf decided it was time to intervene. He stood up to address the group, but his injuries reminded him that he wasn't altogether healed. He waited for the argumentative few to settle down before speaking.

"I have listened to all your suggestions and have weighed each of them carefully and with respect. While I'm grateful for the outpouring of collaboration and support from each of you, I wish to utilize what has always proved successful to me in the past—cunning and stealth. Given that the enemy we face is but a meager few, there is no need for the entire settlement to go traipsing into the frozen north. You have families that need you here. I need but a half-dozen men."

Snorri stood immediately. "I'm in."

"As am I," Jørgen stated without hesitation. All of Gustaf's loyal seven stood up from their benches and willingly accepted the call, Øyven included.

"Øyven, sit down," Gustaf commanded respectively.

"I will not. I deserve to go just as any other."

"And what will your weapon of choice be, boy?" Snorri jibed. "A bird?"

"I'm certain Ketill will lend me his sword," Øyven suggested.

"Think again, Øyven." Ketill stood beside Jørgen. "If my father goes, I go too."

"And I," Ulfr said enthusiastically.

Snorri huffed, displaying his irritation. "See what you've done, Øyven?"

"I have done naught but stand beside my chieftain, which is more than I can say for you." Øyven pointed at Snorri first, then to Jørgen, then a few more around the table. "You all gave up on Gustaf. Erecting a *langskip* for his death when the man's heart still beat in his chest."

Caught unaware by this revelation, Gustaf directed his attention toward Jørgen and Snorri and widened his eyes in astonishment.

"And who rode out each day, looking for Æsa?" Øyven added. "Did you? Or you?" he asked, indicating the six around him. "Nay, 'twas I who searched tirelessly for her. If anyone deserves to go, 'tis I."

Gustaf placed his hand on Øyven's shoulder and nodded. "'Tis true. You've earned a say in this, more so than anyone. But Snorri brings up a good argument. What can you and your bird do for Æsa?"

"My falcon can find her."

Snorri threw back his head and laughed heartily.

"I speak the truth," Øyven insisted. "My falcon can locate Æsa for you, Gustaf. I know she can."

"We haven't the time for childish games, Øyven," Snorri reprimanded.

Gustaf elbowed Snorri. "Enough. Let him speak. Go on, Øyven. I'm listening."

Øyven explained how instinctively the falcon had sought out Æsa in the open meadow, even when she had nothing with which to bait it. "I know Mæva can do this. She will find Æsa and lead us to her. Please, trust me. What have you got to lose, m'lord? If the bird fails, you're no worse off than you are now."

"You're not seriously considering this, are you?" Snorri asked.

"A ruthless bastard has my dearest Æsa. Make no mistake, he'll kill her if she fails to show him where the silver is buried in Tromsø. I've significant reasons for finding her before Asmundr grows impatient, if he hasn't already, for she carries my son in her womb." A rush of muttered reactions filtered across the table, but he continued. "My options are few. I can scour the whole valley of Tromsø until I find her, or slash precious time and release the bird once we arrive. Unless you have a better idea, Øyven and his bird go with us."

****

Æsa retched up the last of her meal in a wooden bucket and sat back on her haunches in exhaustion. For several days, she'd been overcome with morning sickness that sometimes lasted long into the night, and to hide the cause of her nausea, she'd claimed to have caught a stomach ailment. The excuse seemed to work for a while, but she knew Asmundr would likely catch on to her ruse or suspect she was merely stalling. It was only a matter of time before he grew impatient and forced her outside the deserted shack to guide him to the silver.

As she'd feared, Asmundr entered the room and sat by the fire to inspect her state of health. The others, who'd resorted to staying clear of her for fear they too would succumb to illness, remained outside. She endured Asmundr's icy stare until she could bear it no more.

"I thank you for giving me time to gather my strength," she said, hoping to use gratefulness as a way to melt the ice around his cold heart. "I fear I grow worse with each day."

"Is that so?" He removed his dagger from his belt and began admiring it. The blade was well-honed and shiny, as if he'd just sharpened it. "Snow begins to fall, Æsa. And the more it blankets the earth, the harder 'twill be to recognize landmarks. Are you certain this is what you want to do?"

"I know I don't want to die." As she labored to speak, her stomach heaved. Unable to hold it back, she vomited anew and spit the remnants of yellow bile from her mouth.

Asmundr growled and sheathed his knife, standing to pace as she tried to settle herself on the hard floor. His strides, measured and deliberate, stomped off a harrowing rhythm in her head. She knew he was doing so only to intimidate her, to make her understand he wasn't above torture.

Afraid he'd employ whatever means necessary, she tried another amiable approach. "I trust you've kept yourself busy while I've been facedown in a pot. Have you enjoyed your visit to your homeland?"

Asmundr accepted her small talk as he paced. "I have. 'Twas nice to visit my mother's grave after all these years."

Fighting another bout of heaves, she pressed on. "How did she die?"

Asmundr's feet came to a halt, and his eyes swiveled in her direction. "My father killed her."

An unsuspecting tinge of pity clutched at her heart. Though she abhorred Asmundr, she knew his coldhearted nature undoubtedly stemmed from being raised by an even more coldhearted sire. She couldn't help thinking he might have turned out differently had he been born into a loving household. "I'm sorry."

"What do you care?" Asmundr barked, resuming his steps to and fro.

"I know how cruel Ragnar was," she said. "I can only imagine the pain you went through as a child, knowing your own flesh and blood murdered your mother."

Asmundr scoffed. "Would you like to know why he killed her?"

Æsa knew the question was completely rhetorical and waited for him to offer up the gruesome details, terrified she'd vomit again because of it.

"He killed her because she tried to protect me. While she was alive, she'd made attempts to dissolve their marriage on the grounds that he was an unfit father and went as far as to plead her case to the annual council. Behind his back, she implored for the help of the neighboring chieftains who met to provide just rulings for public disputes and private affairs. In fact, Gustaf's father, Rælik, was one of those who ruled in her favor."

He paused for effect, then continued. "After their divorce, Ragnar killed her but made it look like a terrible accident, then pretended to be the grieving husband. He even erected a beautifully carved rune stone in her honor so no one would suspect him of murder. Incidentally, when Harald Fairhair petitioned him and nine others to get rid of a few powerful and persuasive chieftains, Rælik included, my father jumped at the chance."

Æsa's stomach now turned over for other reasons. It was bad enough she shared a bed with the man who'd killed Gustaf's father, but to know Ragnar played such a personal part in Rælik's demise sent her insides into a hot burn. She heaved one more time.

Asmundr watched her struggle but kept on anyway. "Knowing my father, he would have gladly done the deed without payment, but he was rewarded nonetheless. And you..." He suddenly dropped to his knees before her and grabbed a handful of her hair, yanking her face from the pot. He pulled his knife from its sheath with his other hand and placed the point of his dagger against her throat. "...will help me find it, or so help me Odin, I'll slit your throat from ear to ear. Do you understand?"

She slowly nodded in hopes he'd release his hold in her hair before she vomited all over his lap.

"Ragnar took everything from me when he killed my mother in cold blood. I deserve to find that silver." Withdrawing his knife, he threw her sideways and marched back outside.

Tears burned in her eyes as she lay on the dirt floor. She curled up in a ball and wrapped her arms around her belly, hugging the tiny baby that lived within.

In that moment, Æsa understood the drastic measures

Asmundr's mother had gone through to protect her son and the sheer terror she must have felt living with Ragnar. A generation later, Æsa now dwelled in that poor woman's shoes as she'd looked her son in the eye, and it all made sense.

For Ragnar, it was not about hiding the silver so no one could find it. It was about vengeance and settling a score. Asmundr claimed to have known his father well, but it seemed she knew him better. She knew exactly where Ragnar had hidden the blood money used to kill Rælik. It was undoubtedly buried alongside Asmundr's mother.

****

A week later, Asmundr burst through the door again, his eyes narrow slits. The light of the morning sun reflected off the bright white snow behind him, piercing Æsa's tired eyes. A gust of cold air filled the already drafty room.

She had difficulty sitting up. Her body was stiff from lying on a hard floor for so long, and her energy was depleted from her constant morning sickness. Whatever scraps of food Asmundr had given her when he felt generous only came back up hours later. For her baby, she tried to keep some nourishment down, but the nausea was so great at times, she'd get sick at even the thought of drinking water.

Asmundr stalked toward her and kicked the bucket across the room. "On your feet, whore. I can wait no more."

With all her might, Æsa labored to sit up, but her tumbling stomach protested. Asmundr snatched a hank of her hair and jerked her upright.

"Enough of this, Æsa. You're not ill."

She wanted to argue differently but thought better. Nothing she could say would make him believe. Her reprieve was over. He dragged her by the hair out the door while the faces of his three men greeted her with guarded stares.

"My lord, she does not look well."

"Shut up, Grimr! She's fine. She is but faking." Fist still buried in her hair, he led her around the dilapidated shack and shoved her toward the wintry blue water of the strait. "See to your ablutions and make it quick."

She trudged through the ankle-deep snow, the frigid air biting into her skin. She pulled her fur cloak more tightly around her and watched her breath hang like fog in the air. The serenity of the snow-covered landscape fortified by towering jagged mountains taunted her. The clear cerulean channel fenced her in. There was no escape.

Conceding that her fate had been sealed, and the odds of surviving Asmundr's wrath were but zero, she crouched at the water's edge and offered up one final prayer to Odin.

As her warm tears began to freeze upon her cheeks, she heard the shrill cry of a bird. Lazily, she gazed up into the sky and saw the outspread wings of a hovering falcon gracefully circling above her. It was a strange and beautiful sight to see a lone bird venture to such a harsh place. No animal in its right mind would migrate north. Food was too scarce or buried in the tundra.

For a moment, she forgot all about Asmundr and continued to watch the path of the gliding raptor. She shadowed her brow with her hand, gazing into the brilliant sky at the silhouetted bird. To her surprise, it dove toward her.

She fell back on her haunches as the falcon flapped and fluttered about wildly. It squawked and beat its wings, trying to perch. With wide eyes, she tentatively held out her hand and offered her arm. The brown and black patterned falcon landed and settled itself on her shoulder.

Æsa knew this falcon, but couldn't believe her eyes. Tied around the bird's skinny leg was a scrap of white embroidered fabric with stitches she'd sewn.

Her gift to Gustaf.

Quickly, before Asmundr noticed, she untied the material and stuffed it in her sleeve. She searched for Øyven but saw no one. No one but Asmundr and his three brutes.

Her heart leapt, and her body trembled uncontrollably. Had Gustaf's men come to save her? She wanted to call out to them but thought better of it.

As she encouraged the falcon to take flight, the thunderous beat of horses' hooves rumbled over the frozen land beneath her. Her breath caught in her lungs upon seeing a swarm of mounted *hirdmen* racing down the hill.

Although helmeted and armed to the teeth, their fierce determination distinguished them as her gallant rescuers.

Asmundr and his men had already begun to scramble. Out of the ten daunting warriors, one drew his bow and took careful aim. The arrow sliced through the air and sank deep into Grimr's shoulder, propelling him onto his backside.

"Stand your ground!" Asmundr bellowed, unsheathing his sword. But like the coward he was, he deserted his men and ran toward Æsa.

She gathered her skirts and tried to forge through the snow, but his legs proved to be faster and stronger. Grabbing her around the waist, he dragged her flailing body back toward the shelter of the shack.

"Get inside!" Asmundr called to Grimr.

Æsa wailed and screamed. She fought to break free of Asmundr's hold, but he was able to haul her weak body back to the shack. Another arrow sank into the outside wall of the house, stopping him in his tracks. He ducked below it and shuffled through the door, shielding himself with Æsa's body. Grimr followed, ordering the last two men to hold their positions, and slammed the door behind him.

Struck with fear, Æsa listened to the sounds on the other side. Shouts, neighing horses, and the clashing of iron resounded through the weathered wood of the shack as if it were but sheer linen. Outnumbered five to one, their struggle to defend the post did not last long. The harrowing screams of dying men was the last thing Æsa heard before

Asmundr jerked her back to the far wall and rammed his knife up under her chin.

"You want to live, Æsa? Then call off Gustaf's men!"

Chapter Twenty-seven

Gustaf stared at the two worthless men who lay dead at his feet. He almost pitied them for their blind servitude to such a selfish coward. Essentially, Asmundr had left them to die, for there was no way a pair of insufficiently armed men could triumph over ten mounted warriors with shields, swords, and bows.

The small victory felt good in his vengeful heart, but it was the success of killing Asmundr he longed to attain. Through the eyeholes of his helmet, he glowered at the rickety door before him and dreaded knowing what had gone on between Æsa and Asmundr behind it.

As he stood brooding, his blood coursed through his veins and a heavy pulse raged in his ears. All the pain he'd felt from his injuries vanished through the adrenaline gushing into his bloodstream. Like a berserker, he was numb from head to toe, cold and hard like the tempered steel of his sword. He felt nothing but sheer fury. His hands shook with it.

In silence, he gestured toward the two dead and motioned for them to be dragged away. Snorri and Ketill obliged, but Jørgen grabbed hold of Gustaf's arm before he prepared to kick open the door.

Keeping his voice low, Jørgen muttered, "Let me do this. You're injured."

"Jørgen?" Æsa's shaky voice came from inside. "Is that you?"

Gustaf heart jumped in his throat, and he nodded toward Jørgen, permitting him to answer.

"Aye, Æsa. 'Tis me. We've come for you."

"Please, do not come in here," she shouted in desperation. "Asmundr promises to kill me if you do."

Her frightened voice sent chills down Gustaf's spine. He knew Asmundr meant what he said.

With a nod, Gustaf encouraged Jørgen to keep her talking, while he signaled the others to surround the place. Each man did as he was bid, working together as experienced warriors who knew how to secure a stronghold.

"Æsa, I'm coming in."

"Nay, Jørgen, nay! Please do as he says! He has a knife…and he will slit my throat. He will! He will! Please!"

Gustaf could stand it no more. He tightened his grip on his sword and kicked open the door. It crashed and splintered to pieces as he stepped inside.

"Watch out!" Æsa cried, trying to warn him of Grimr, who lurked in the shadows.

Gustaf took a blow to the head and fell to his knees, the sound of Grimr's sword echoing like a loud clang inside his helmet. He shook it off and tackled the man around his knees. The two tumbled to the floor, throwing punches in a wild frenzy, but Gustaf soon gained the upper hand. He rolled on top and sent a solid fist straight into the man's nose.

Blood spewed as Grimr fought to defend himself.

In a battle to regain their swords, they sprawled across the floor and grappled to recover their weapons before the other. They jumped to their feet, and iron clashed in a frantic effort to hack their opponent in two. Gustaf dodged a decapitating blow and spun, slicing Grimr's thigh wide open.

The man collapsed and writhed in pain. Æsa's cry of terror pierced Gustaf's ears, but he paid no heed. He double fisted his sword above his head and delivered the fatal thrust through Grimr's heart.

Swiveling his head, he set his sights on Asmundr, who had already begun to make threats upon Æsa. He watched as the dagger inched closer under her jaw, the blade depressing her delicate skin.

"Jørgen," Asmundr warned, adjusting his body behind Æsa's. "Think about what you're doing. One move in my direction, and I'll spill her blood!"

Gustaf scoffed inside, enjoying the fact Asmundr had no idea who he was talking to. Like a fool, he believed him to be Jørgen and that Gustaf was dead and gone from this earth.

"I mean what I say, Jørgen. Put your sword down!"

"I haven't a sword," Jørgen interrupted from the open

doorway behind Gustaf, his bow nocked and drawn. Without hesitation, he released the arrow.

Asmundr cried out as it pierced the shoulder left exposed. He staggered backward, his blade no longer a threat. Æsa fell to the floor in a heap and scrambled to get away from him.

Gustaf rushed to her and pulled her to her feet. "Get her out of here," he commanded Jørgen.

Upon hearing his voice, Æsa widened her eyes in recognition. Uncontrollable joy mixed with untamed fear crossed her face as Jørgen grabbed her by the waist and hauled her outside to safety.

Gustaf drew his attention back to Asmundr, who actually had the audacity to unsheathe his sword with an inept left hand, and approached him. Gustaf could see that in his panicked state he was still wondering who was behind the helmet. With one swipe of his sword, he disarmed Asmundr and forced him to his knees, holding the tip of his blade at Asmundr's sternum. Only then did he removed his helmet and toss it aside.

"It cannot be," Asmundr muttered in utter bewilderment. "But how? Grimr killed you."

Gustaf glanced back at Grimr's dead body. It was apparent Asmundr, still in shock, was clueless to the obvious. "As you can see, Grimr tried twice and failed both times."

"Wait!" Asmundr spat as soon as Gustaf readied his sword for the final plunge. "The silver! I'll let you have it. It can all be yours."

Gustaf scoffed, appalled that even as Asmundr looked death in the eye, he thought he could barter his way free with his own father's blood money. Gustaf refused to give this eel scum the satisfaction of a reply. Instead, he adjusted his hands on the grip.

The man trembled as he realized Gustaf's intent. Perspiration broke out above his brow, and his breaths came in deep, sporadic huffs. "Surely there is some mercy left in your soul, Gustaf. A fragment of temperance, perhaps?"

Gustaf froze upon the word choice. His mind swarmed with images of Æsa stroking his temple, kissing his lips, and whispering her pet name in his ears. The sound of her sweet voice melted the tension from his rigid body.

But his visions soon turned heinous. Her cries of pain, her screams of terror all reminded him of what this bastard had done to her. And what he'd done to him, all for the sake of greed.

He looked Asmundr in the eye and said, "If I've any temperance left, know 'tis only reserved for those who deserve it." And with one final thrust, Gustaf ended his torment. Asmundr's body flinched when the broad blade speared through his chest. Bones snapped and blood gushed from his mouth. Justice had been served.

Gustaf placed his booted foot upon Asmundr's lifeless corpse and withdrew his weapon, closing his eyes to the wicked image in his head.

"Gustaf!" Æsa called from behind him.

Slowly, he looked at her. Her clothes were tattered and torn. Her face was pale, highlighting an ugly bruise on her left eye. Her lips were chapped and her hair fell around her shoulders in a tangled, matted mess. Gustaf was never so happy to see his beautiful, dearest Æsa.

He ran to her and swept her up in his arms, burying his face in her hair as he held her close. During his long journey to find her, he feared he'd not be blessed with this moment. That he might be too late to save her and the unborn child in her womb. Breathing her in and feeling her tight embrace around his neck proved he'd won the day.

He hoped his father looked down on him with pride.

Chapter Twenty-eight

The journey back to Dal Hinna Dauðu was a daunting one. Winter had come early and with its arrival came strong cold winds and incessant snowfall. Gustaf and the nine others did their best to accommodate Æsa, stopping as frequently as possible to allow her to rest and, at times, vomit in privacy. But time was of the essence if they wanted to get safely home and not freeze to death in the tundra.

For a fortnight, they traveled through the harshest conditions. Food was scarce, and it seemed most game had taken refuge from the storm. Any edible vegetation was covered with a hard crust of snow. Rationing what little they had in their reserves became pertinent to their survival.

Starving and frozen to the bone, Æsa snuggled close to Gustaf's chest as they continued to press on. Tiny icicles clung to her eyelashes and wet snowflakes burned her reddened cheeks. Huddling deep beneath their snow-dusted bearskin cloaks for warmth, she couldn't recall a time when she'd ever been this cold. She tried not to complain, but her shivering and growling belly often reminded Gustaf in her stead.

Finally, after three weeks of total misery, they arrived home. The generous villagers crowded around them, happy and relieved their loved ones had made it back home uninjured. All extended their services, from caring for the spent horses to providing hot soups and stews to their famished friends. Everyone contributed, but Gustaf saw to Æsa's needs before his own.

He dismounted in haste and carried her into Halldora's home, where he stripped her of her sodden clothing. Æsa could barely lift a finger to help as she had no energy to lift a muscle. As soon as he laid her down and covered her with a pile of warm furs, he tore off his own clothes and snuggled in behind her. Together they lay beneath the blankets, letting the roaring fire warm them.

Gustaf rubbed her arms, her legs, her back, trying to use friction to ward away the chill from her goose-pimpled flesh. The warmth of his hard-muscled body wrapped around her gave her comfort knowing she was safe from Asmundr's cruelty.

When she'd heard Gustaf's voice, after believing for so long that he was dead, she nearly died of shock. The gods must have heard her prayers and delivered him unto her in her time of great need. How could she be so fortunate now when all her life she'd been countlessly forsaken?

Like a gusty storm, Halldora entered and eyed the two shivering bodies in her boxbed. She stoked the fire and began rummaging around the shelves, looking through her assorted vials and jars of stones.

"Do not rush me, Gustaf," Halldora scolded as she heard his thoughts. "I'm doing what I can to help Æsa."

"Forget me," Æsa said, her lower lip quivering. "How is the babe?"

"You need to eat, child. A brew of meadwort, goldenrod, and hop will ease your nausea. And hold your tongue, warrior. I cannot think when you're badgering me with your complaints and worries. Trust in me for once." She took the herbs she had in store and measured them carefully before putting them into a mortar made of wood. Using a pestle, she crushed the ingredients then tapped them out onto several sheets of cheesecloth. She tied it up and placed the filtered bag into a pot of steaming water at the fire.

"Halldora, please," Gustaf said impatiently. "The babe. How does my son fare?"

Halldora turned from the fire in agitation. "The babe's heart is weak."

"Then do something!" Gustaf snapped.

"I am, you overgrown ox." She retrieved a smooth, reddish stone from one of her jars and tied a string around it. She lifted the fur at Æsa's stomach and placed her hands upon her belly. Halldora cringed and made haste to fasten the rock to one of Æsa's thighs, but Gustaf stopped her.

"What is that?"

"'Tis a jasper stone."

"My Æsa is not in need of pretty jewelry."

"You want your son to be born before 'tis time?"

Halldora barked. "Your Æsa's womb contracts as we speak. The stone will stop her labor. Remove your hand."

"Gustaf, please," Æsa encouraged. "Let her do what she must."

Reluctantly, Gustaf allowed the old woman access but continued to stare. "You blame me for this, witch, do you not?"

Halldora rolled her eyes. "You did all you could. Now, let me do what I do best." She reached up and felt Æsa's neck, face, and chest. "Your body heat is not aiding her enough. Get dressed and fetch me a cauldron of hot water."

"I'm not leaving her."

"You'll do as I say, Gustaf."

The look Halldora flashed him was not one that any intelligent man would ignore. No one really knew what the frail old woman was capable of when it came to her talents, but then again, no one in his right mind would dare provoke her. Gustaf was no different.

With a huff, he sat up. "Would it be too much to ask for a little privacy?"

Halldora waved him off. "You forget I've seen all there is to see when I began preparing your body for the afterlife. I'm certain your precious manhood still resembles a flaccid eel. Now, be off with you."

Æsa hid her smile as the two battled it out with glares and groans. Gustaf tore himself from the boxbed and drove his limbs back into his clothes, then left the hut, slamming the door behind him.

Halldora gave Æsa a grin of satisfaction. "My, he is a stubborn one."

Æsa couldn't argue but stood up for him nonetheless. "That stubborn man just saved my life."

"And we must save this child." Halldora dipped a ladle into the brewing potion and held it before Æsa's lips. The potent smell accosted her nose.

"Drink...for the babe."

Æsa sipped the bitter liquid. The acrid taste lingered on her tongue as it flowed down her throat, making her want to gag. After a few more difficult swallows, the nausea started to subside. She looked at Halldora gratefully. Not just for taking care of her, but for nursing her dying Gustaf back to life.

"Don't thank me, Æsa. Instead, you should thank Gustaf for his strength and courage. A weaker man would have died after what I put him through. You mean everything to him and, for that, he'll be a suitable husband and father—an overly-protective husband and father, I might add."

"I would not want him any other way." Æsa smiled, giving thought to Gustaf holding their newborn son in his arms. It was a pleasant image as her eyelids drooped, and, before she could stop the fluttering, she drifted off to sleep.

****

"Æsa," Gustaf said sweetly, stroking her hair from her face. "Æsa, wake up."

Her eyelids fluttered but never fully opened. He could tell she was utterly exhausted and feared her arms and legs were still too cool to the touch.

Determined to warm her thoroughly, he slipped his arms beneath her and picked her up. Her naked body, bejeweled with a single stone around her thigh, lay draped in his arms and he couldn't help but think the worst.

"Please, Æsa. Open your eyes."

Again her eyes fluttered. Her hand touched his bare chest, and a tiny smile inched up in one corner of her mouth. "Your skin is warm."

"And yours is not."

He carried her over to a large caldron of steaming water and stepped inside. Glorious heat surrounded his aching calves, then his thighs as he lowered himself. Æsa stirred as they lowered into the bath together, the sudden warmth taking her breath away. She clung to him at first, as if the hot water were painful to endure, but slowly relaxed upon his lap. Her head fell against his chest, and her arms snuggled around his lower back.

Submerged to their shoulders, Gustaf held her weakened body in a tight embrace. He didn't care that his stomach growled with hunger or that his body craved sleep. All that concerned him was his dearest Æsa and the son she carried. She couldn't lose this baby. She just couldn't.

"Where is Halldora?" Æsa asked in a raspy whisper.

"I sent her away."

Æsa's breath brushed past his wet skin as if she attempted to laugh. "And she allowed it?"

"I threatened to warm you the way a man knows best."

"Surely, Halldora saw your true thoughts on the matter."

"Who said 'twas not in my thoughts? When it comes to you, love, 'tis not difficult to imagine my body joined with yours at any given moment."

He felt her hand shove him playfully. "I lack the strength to even think of such an act."

"And the strength to fight me off, I'd imagine."

Her cute little giggle lifted his spirits. Truth be told, he lacked the energy to do much more than hold her in his arms, but it was his overactive imagination that kept the old woman away and that suited him just fine.

"How do you feel?" he finally asked. "Can you eat?"

"I can try."

"'Twould give me hope if you would." He reached across the caldron and took the ladle that rested in a pot of boiled shallots, cabbage, and bear meat. He held the savory soup to her lips. "Eat, Æsa. Come on."

In small sips, she took in the broth. He knew she was doing all she could to tolerate the food. It pleased him when she slowly consumed about three spoonfuls. In between helping her, he devoured some of the warm, meaty soup until they each had their fill. If Halldora was anything, she was a good cook.

With his hunger finally satiated, he tossed the wooden utensil back into the pot and let his head rest against the rim of the caldron. Lost in his thoughts, he absently cupped handfuls of oil-scented water over her shoulder.

"What worries you, m'lord?"

"Many things," he admitted.

She sighed and snuggled closer. "Talk to me, Gustaf."

He closed his eyes and adjusted his arms around her. "I worry that too much strain has been placed on our son. Halldora says he fights to live."

"And that he will," Æsa reassured him. "He is a strong warrior like his father. I can feel it. But the baby is not the only thing that troubles you, is it?"

Gustaf grumbled. He didn't like that Æsa, even in her tired state, could sense his innermost worries. He would rather have kept them to himself. "Winter has come, which means we must wait out the season before sailing to Inishmore."

"What is wrong with that, m'lord?"

"I had hopes that I'd be amongst my family when my son was born."

Æsa's hand came out of the water and caressed his face. Her brilliant eyes regarded him with sympathy and compassion. "You needn't worry, Gustaf. The babe is not due until late spring. We shall sail for Inishmore at the first sign of winter breaking, and your family will witness this birth, as long as the gods will it."

"That is what concerns me most, Æsa. From the time

we first met, we've been allotted naught but headaches and peril." Gustaf averted his gaze from her. "I almost lost you. I know not what I would've done had something happened to you."

Æsa cupped his face. "I thought I lost you as well. But we are here—together. Safe in each other's arms because of your bravery. You saved us, Gustaf. Remember that."

He tried to hold fast to that thought, but whenever he recalled how he'd saved Æsa, Asmundr's ugly face tainted the otherwise rewarding vision. It bothered him most that Asmundr, the son of the man who killed his own father, had once bested him.

His head hurt from the regrets he retained, despite his victory. He closed his eyes and let his head fall back again. "Enough talk. I just want to hold you." He drew in a long breath and released it. "Oh, Æsa, you're all I need in this wretched world."

Chapter Twenty-nine

Five months later
Early spring, 924 A.D.

An unseasonably warm wind blew off the Atlantic, melting the snow and ice on the lowlands. Budding vegetation blossomed under the morning sun. Shimmering dew clung to the fresh green foliage. It was a beautiful day to start a journey. A promising life of peace and tranquility awaited Gustaf and Æsa as they made their way south to Oslofjord through the petty kingdom of Viken.

All of Gustaf's men, Halldora, Helga, Jørgen's two sons, and several loyal servants accompanied them to the bay. The small longship that had been prematurely built for Gustaf's journey into the Otherworld was now going to be utilized to sail him and Æsa to Inishmore. Constructed of heavy oak, the vessel was dragged across the land beneath rolling timbers manned by *thralls*.

Sleds pulled by horses carried extravagant marriage gifts, newly woven clothing, chests of oils, spices, and jewelry, and food reserves. The generosity among the people was incomprehensible as they offered masses of wares to their departing friends.

It was difficult for Gustaf to accept their overabundance of hospitality, but he didn't put up much of a fight, for it was considered rude and offensive to deny the openhandedness of others. He could only look back at the caravan of cargo trailing behind him and feel blessed to have known such hospitable people. If not for his family that awaited his return on Inishmore, he would have been content to stay and raise his children among them.

Ignoring the tug on his heart, Gustaf led his horse down the grassy slope on foot. He would have preferred to ride behind Æsa, but with her belly swollen with child, there was no room in the saddle to accommodate them both.

Once they reached the bottom, the longship was placed in the water and loaded. Extra care had been taken to balance the cargo within the hull to ensure the vessel wouldn't capsize once the crew boarded. Chests, doubling as benches, lined each side of the boat, where an equal division of Gustaf's men would row the oars. A solid pine mast lay at their feet until conditions were right for raising the sail on the open sea. Confirming the buoyancy of the ship, six slender oars were slotted into the oarholes and the rigging secured. Their longship, adorned with intricate carvings along the gunwale and prow, sat proudly adrift on the shoreline as the water lapped against its streamlined sides.

Gustaf gazed at his well-crafted ship and his seven

loyal men ready to cast away with him as they'd done so many times before. A sense of wistful sentiment and pride overtook him. They were brothers by oath and warriors by blood. He could think of no better friends than those who aimed to see him start his newfound life as a future husband and father.

He turned to Æsa and lifted her from the horse's back. Setting her on her feet, he held her close and cradled her protruding belly with his hand. "Are you certain you're ready for this?"

"If you're asking me if I'm ready to meet your family at last and take you as my husband, then aye." She stretched her aching back as she braced herself with his forearm. "And more importantly, the sooner we marry, the sooner I can birth this temperamental boy. I swear he's going to kick and scream his way out."

Gustaf laughed and slid his hand down her thigh until he found the jasper stone Halldora had fastened to her leg many months ago. "You keep him in there for a little while longer, you hear?"

"As best I can," Æsa groaned.

He picked her up and carried her to the side of the longship, where Jørgen and his sons gathered to exchange words and hearty embraces. Gustaf handed her to Snorri and waited until he set her safely on the chest near the steerboard before he turned to say his own farewells.

Ulfr met him halfway with a large bundle across his arms. Ketill crowded behind him. Gustaf examined how neatly it was secured with leather straps. "What is this?"

"'Tis a gift from Ketill and myself," Ulfr explained. "But you must promise not to open it until after the birth of your son." Ketill stepped forward and dropped a heavy hand upon Gustaf's shoulder. "It has been an honor, m'lord, to hunt and take up arms with you. Know that you'll always be welcome amongst us, son of Rælik."

"That means a great deal to me." Gustaf glanced at Halldora and Helga waiting in the distance. "Watch over them as you have always done. That is all I ask." He also noticed the tinge of sadness in the sons' faces, knowing their father was leaving them again. "Your father will return before the summer solstice. I give you my word."

He gave each strapping lad a vigorous embrace and made his way toward the two women who insisted on seeing them off. He took Helga's hand and gave it a reassuring squeeze. "Øyven will be back before you know it. This I swear." He could sense, as she kept glancing over his shoulder, that she was most eager to say a personal good-bye to the handsome warrior. "Go on. Say your farewells."

Helga, in a fit of excitement, sprinted down the hill toward the ship. He watched as Øyven leapt over the side of the longship and ran to meet her, throwing his arms around her.

When Gustaf looked back at Halldora, he was surprised to see the old woman smiling instead of grimacing. "'Tis a good match," he asserted.

Halldora gave him a sideways glance. "You need not convince me, Gustaf. I know well the happiness Øyven has brought my granddaughter."

"'Tis nigh killing you, is it not?"

"What?"

"That you cannot hear what they are thinking or saying to each other right now."

"Don't taunt me, warrior."

Gustaf tugged the old woman into his arms and hugged her. "It does you good to step into a world blind and deaf to others' emotions from time to time. Cherish the silence whilst you have it."

"I assure you 'tis nice to have reprieve from *your* lustful thoughts for a change."

"Serves you right, Halldora. I told you many times to stay out of my head."

Halldora shook hers and rolled her eyes. "Be off with you."

"You're going to miss me," Gustaf interjected playfully. Like a lively lad whose enthusiasm got the better of him, Gustaf jogged past Øyven and slapped him on the back, interrupting his private conversation with Helga. "With or without you."

"I'm coming," Øyven said. He gazed one last time into Helga's beautiful eyes. "I will return."

Helga smiled shyly. "I will wait for you. And worry

not. I'll take proper care of your falcon."

He cupped her hands in his. "I've no doubts."

Helga wiped away a falling tear and took out a scabbard and sword from within her cloak. She traced her fingers along the leather sheath, eyeing the shiny silver hilt decorated with amber stones extending beyond the casing. "I want you to have this. 'Twas my father's."

Øyven's gaze dropped to the beautiful weapon. "I cannot accept such a gift."

"You will. I insist." She looked down at her feet nervously. "I must know you're safe. Please, take it."

Øyven grasped the weapon reverently in both hands and slid the blade halfway out, inspecting the craftsmanship. He sheathed it in haste and secured it at his hip. "I'm not worthy to possess your father's sword, but I'm honored nonetheless."

Before he could say more, Helga reached up on tiptoes and planted a quick kiss on his lips. She gathered her skirts and ran back toward her grandmother.

Øyven stood there in shock. He touched his mouth and smiled, the feel of her kiss lingering as he watched her climb the hill.

Snorri cleared his throat purposely loud from within the ship and gained the young man's attention. Upon seeing the longship floating out to sea, Øyven waded through ankle-deep waters and hoisted himself over the side, falling awkwardly to his knees. He ignored the insults and jests that greeted him and stared back across the water at the only woman who'd enchanted his heart.

"Man your oar, boy," Snorri commanded from his post. "And I'm not talking about the one between your legs. Count your blessings that Halldora is unaware of your *rising* interest in her granddaughter."

Øyven settled himself at the only empty chest and gripped the oar with both hands. "So, it comes back to this, aye? Cutting me down to size for your gain?"

"You should know better than to bring your feelings with you, Øyven."

"Odin's teeth, here we go again," Jørgen sighed, casting an apologetic look toward Æsa. "I fear 'twill be a long journey for you, m'lady."

She glanced over her shoulder at Gustaf who stood fixed at the steer board behind her. "Is this what you had to listen to all these years?"

"Every bit of it, love."

Æsa cradled her stomach and rubbed the active babe within. "My word, Gustaf. 'Tis a wonder you had any temperance left."

Chapter Thirty

Æsa doubled over, groaning and panting through the onset of labor as the longship tossed about on the waves. Her contractions began to occur at regular intervals, spurring Gustaf into frantic haste. Between ordering his men to row harder and intermittently giving up his post at the stern to talk her through the agony, he assumed many tasks to get the mother of his child safely to land before she gave birth on the open sea.

Gustaf scanned the horizon and spotted the much-desired island of Inishmore. "Heave, men! I'll not have my son born on this bloody ship!"

Racked with pain, Æsa groaned and slipped off the bench to recline on the hardened planks of the hull. "Gustaf…"

He deserted the steer board and fell to his knees beside her, taking her hand. He watched as she bent her legs in a birthing position, her thighs spread apart. In haste, he blocked any view his men might have with skirts and pulled them down over her calves.

"You cannot have this baby now, Æsa."

She glowered at him, her eyes as blazing as the hair

upon her head. "I don't think I have a choice in the matter," she gritted through clenched teeth. Another moan escaped her, and Gustaf's chest tightened.

Without thinking, he cupped her mound and pressed his palm against her. Again her eyes glared at him like heated embers. "You think you can hold the babe in?"

The idiocy of his actions hit him as sharply as Æsa's sarcastic remark. He knew no matter what he tried, his son would soon be born on this earth, with or without his consent. "Tell me what to do."

"Tell your men to turn around! I'll not have them staring at me while this baby emerges from my—" Her words were cut off by another excruciating contraction. The shrill sound of her cry sliced through the wooden hull of the crowded longship and echoed over the Atlantic.

Gustaf sat frozen, helpless, staring at her dilated private parts. Æsa sat up in a flash and grabbed him by the cloak, jerking his face toward hers. "Turn. Your men. Around!"

Gustaf shook himself out of his incapacitating stupor and swiveled his head on his shoulders, meeting the wide-eyed stares of his rowing men. "You heard the woman. Turn around! Assume a raid-retreat position and heave for all you're worth!"

"But, m'lord," Snorri said, still dazed. "'Twill be more difficult—"

"Snorri!" Æsa screamed, yanking Gustaf's dagger from his belt and brandishing its shiny blade. "'Twill be more difficult for you to row without your bollocks!"

Immediately, all seven warriors cupped their cherished testicles and spun on their benches. By pushing the oars away from their bodies, they propelled the streamlined vessel headlong toward the rocky isle. No one dared test the authority of the hostile woman in labor lest she act upon her threat.

"Easy now, Æsa," Gustaf soothed, carefully confiscating the knife from her trembling hand. "Settle yourself."

Æsa's face puckered with a hatred he'd never seen before. "Settle myself?"

Gustaf stammered, realizing he'd said the wrong thing. "I—I mean—"

"I'm about to push your whale-sized son out an opening the size of my nostril and you want me to settle myself?"

Gustaf glanced down between her legs. "If you could see what I see, you'd not exactly regard it as a small opening."

Unamused, she sat up and grabbed his crotch in her fist. "If you do not get me off this ship, I swear I will geld you myself."

He tried to pry her fingers open and nodded. "I'll get you to land. Just, for the love of Odin, release me."

Fortunately for him, she fell victim to another contraction and she then clutched her tightening stomach. Gustaf dropped backward and supported his throbbing genitals in his palm. He didn't dare complain about his dull ache or the fact that he thought he might vomit his bollocks at her feet. Only a foolish man would mention his misery when his woman was writhing in childbirth.

When he fell in love with Æsa for her feisty spirit and quick temper, this wasn't exactly the kind of vivaciousness he had in mind. Never in all his years did he think he'd be enchanted by a feminine hellhound who looked like a goddess and screamed like a banshee. Nonetheless, he loved her with all his heart and reminded himself that his lovely betrothed would return to him as soon as she delivered the baby.

He scrambled to his haunches and commanded his men with a strained voice. "Row like you have never rowed before, men. Trust me when I tell you, your lives depend on it."

When he looked back at Æsa, he saw that tears streamed from her eyes as she lay on her back, staring at the gray sky above. Pity overtook him and he crawled to her side, wiping the trail of wetness from her temples. "We are almost there, Æsa. Hold on, love." He took hold of her hand and held it tightly. "I'll not leave your side."

"It hurts…"

"I know," Gustaf soothed, squeezing her hand. "But 'twill soon be over. And we'll have a son. Do not cry, my dearest Æsa." He looked ahead, checking the distance of the approaching north shore of Inishmore. "Row!" he bellowed.

****

The longship dragged keel upon the rocky shoreline of the isle, and Gustaf jumped to his feet. As he suspected, Tait, his late brother's best friend, and Nevan, the Irish king of the isle, ran into the rough surf to assist them.

He braced himself across the gunwale to shelter Æsa and called out orders while his men leapt from the sides to drag the boat inland.

"Gustaf!" Tait exclaimed with joy. "You've returned."

"Quick! Æsa is in labor!"

Tait and Nevan peered into the hull and saw the woman sprawled across the planks. "Dear, Lord," Nevan muttered as Æsa howled.

Tait grabbed the king's arm. "Fetch Mara and Lillemor. Hurry!"

Gustaf bent and picked her up in his arms, jumping into the shallow water of the pebbled beach. Æsa wailed, and he locked eyes with Tait. "Where do I take her?"

"Mara's. This way." They ran to Mara's longhouse, and Tait burst through her door. Breandán, Mara's new husband, stood up in surprise from his work crafting arrows and recognized Dægan's eldest brother. "Good to see you again, Gustaf. Who might this be?"

"This is Æsa," Tait introduced. "Gustaf's wife. And she's in labor."

Gustaf corrected Tait. "She's not my wife. But she will

be. I wanted to wait and marry her amongst my family and then have the baby, but it seems my son has different plans."

"Gustaf," Æsa said sweetly, now that she was between contractions. "I want to marry now."

He looked at her in his arms. "I don't think there's time, and—"

Æsa stiffened and shrieked in pain as another contraction ripped through her. "Please, Gustaf! I don't want my son to be born a bastard!"

Gustaf looked between Tait and Breandán. "You heard the woman. Get one of your holy men down here and have him marry us."

"You realize he's a Christian man," Tait said warily. "Of the cloth. It goes against his religion to marry you under your Norse gods. He'll not do it."

"Then marry us under Christ or whatever name by which He's known. I care not."

"'Tis not that simple, Gustaf," Tait stated.

Gustaf laid Æsa on the nearest boxbed, then grabbed the front of Tait's kirtle and gave him a quick shake. "It *is* that simple, Tait. Make it happen, I beg you."

"What's all the noise about?" Mara asked as she came in the door. "Oh, Gustaf. You've returned," she said in surprise. Nevan and Lillemor followed her inside as she skirted the many people who'd filled her spacious longhouse.

Gustaf rushed toward her. "Mara, I need you to

convince the Irish priest that he is to marry Æsa and me. Under your god. Please."

"At this moment?" she asked, noting the vulnerable condition Æsa was in as she lay there sweating, panting, and moaning. "But Æsa is about to have a baby."

"I know," Gustaf said exasperated. "But she wants to be married before. If 'tis important to her, then 'tis important to me." He clutched her arms for emphasis. "Please, Mara. You know how much this means to me. How much 'twould mean to Dægan." He didn't mean to throw his deceased brother in her face, but he found himself resorting to desperate measures. He dropped to his knees. "Please. Please help me."

Mara took one look at the mighty warrior at her feet and surrendered. "Tait, go quickly. Bring the priest as fast as you can."

Tait sprinted from the longhouse without question, and soon everyone was doing as they were bid. Mara was the daughter of the Irish king, and no one hesitated to meet her demands.

Gustaf threw his arms around her waist and hugged her before standing. "I thank you, my lady."

"'Tis not done yet," she murmured, leaving Gustaf to join Æsa at her bedside. "How are you doing?"

Æsa answered with a pitiful nod and a fake smile.

Mara brushed back her hair and spoke reassuringly to the spent woman. "I need to see how close you are. All right?" Gustaf came to Æsa'a side and grasped her hand.

Mara regarded the ridiculous number of men around her hearth who gathered like foraging hens. "Everyone out. You too, Gustaf."

"I'm not leaving her."

"This is no place for a man."

Gustaf leaned in and didn't budge from his statement. "Try to throw me out, princess."

Mara sighed. "You Rælik sons are a stubborn lot. Fine. You can stay. But you'll do as I say. Æsa will need you to be strong. Can you do that?"

"I'm not afraid of the sight of blood, if that's what you mean."

"'Tis one thing to see the spilled blood of your enemies, Gustaf. 'Tis quite another to see it spill from the woman you love." Without another word on the matter, she directed Lillemor to boil water at the hearth and bring a stack of clean linen. "Gustaf, your task is to make certain Æsa is comfortable. Whatever she needs."

"I can do that," he said with confidence.

"And what do I do?" Æsa asked meekly.

Mara smiled and got into position between her bent knees. "For now, you just rest. In time, you're going to need all your strength to push this child out." She reached inside Æsa and felt the baby's head in the birth canal.

Gustaf stared, his mind in a whirlwind. He couldn't believe what he'd just seen. The door opened and Tait's eyes widened. He immediately turned around and apologized. "Gustaf. May I have a word with you—

anywhere but here?"

Gustaf grumbled and sped after Tait, who had already left. As he stepped beyond the door, a sea of anxious eyes gawked at him. It appeared as if the entire isle, Celt and Northmen alike, had come to await the birth of his son at the threshold of Mara's longhouse.

Tait ushered him forward, speaking low as they walked through the mass of people. "He wants to meet you first."

Gustaf caught sight of the holy man dressed in orthodox brown wool with a string of large wooden beads hanging around his forearm. He ignored the introduction Tait tried to provide and broke in, "You'll marry us, aye?"

Nervously, the docile monk withstood the intimidating stance of the large warrior before him, having to lift his chin in order to look Gustaf in the eyes. "Is it your wish to forsake your pagan gods and follow the one true god, your Creator and Father?"

"If 'twill get you in there quicker, then, aye."

"This should not be a hasty decision on your part, my son. To follow God means to know Him and feel Him in your heart."

Gustaf ripped his dagger from his belt and shoved the point of the blade beneath the priest's chin. "Do you feel that, holy man?"

Tait and Nevan immediately intervened and took hold of Gustaf's arms, talking him down. "This is not the way to get what you want."

"Sure 'tis. Look at him. He knows his life hangs in the

balance."

The monk swallowed tentatively. "'Tis all right, Tait. He speaks the truth, and I'm not a foolish man. There is passion in his words and, strangely enough, the good Lord suffered the same at Gethsemane."

Gustaf pulled the priest closer by his clothes. "Is that an aye?"

Tait and Nevan reaffirmed their hold on his arms, though they did little to inhibit him from running the priest through should it have come to that.

The holy man cleared his throat and, with his free hand, gently plucked the weapon from Gustaf's hand. "As I told your brother Dægan once, when he insisted upon using force to enter the house of God, humility and kindness go much further than hostility and aggression when one is in need."

Gustaf shrugged Tait and Nevan from his arms. "I was told my brother died a Christian man."

"Aye, he accepted God into his heart," the monk said. "Of his own free will, I might add."

"Then, like my brother, I shall do the same." Gustaf bowed his head and caught sight of the silver pagan amulet swinging from his own belt. Proving his sincerity to forsake his heathen ways, he tore Thor's hammer from his hip, brandished it for all to see, and tossed the sentimental trinket into the distant lapping ocean. "There. I renounce my gods. Is that good enough?" A cry from inside Mara's home erupted through the silence, and he could barely contain himself. He fell to one knee and bowed his head before speaking. "For the love of all things holy, just what must I do to convince you?" He thumped his chest with his fist. "I swear I sever all ties with my war god. May Thor strike me dead if it pleases you."

"Enough. On your feet. I will do as you ask, for God welcomes all—even the wolves that pasture with the sheep. But," the monk warned, pointing at Tait, "I leave the responsibility of properly converting this Northman in your hands."

Tait nodded reluctantly.

"Shall we?" the monk gestured.

Gustaf ran ahead of him and blocked the door before letting him through. "You may want to cover your eyes before you enter."

Tait patted the priest's shoulder. "Trust me. You'll be grateful you did."

Confused, the monk brought his hands up to his face and covered his eyes. With Gustaf's guidance, he was led into the longhouse, the shriek of a woman in labor piercing his ears.

Gustaf led the man around the hearth to Æsa's head and quickly knelt beside her. "I'm here, my love," he said, wiping her brow with a cool cloth.

"We've not much time, Gustaf," Mara said. "Once the baby descends, Æsa must push."

Gustaf jerked the priest closer by his arm. "You heard the princess. Proceed."

The distraught monk cleared his throat and commenced the unconventional ceremony with the conventional Latin introduction. "*In nomine Patris et Filii et Spiritus Sancti. Amen.*"

From then on, Gustaf was oblivious to the man behind him who recited words of unknown purpose. He was attentive only to his suffering Æsa, making certain he did all that Mara asked of him.

He may have failed to protect her from Asmundr, but he'd not fail her now. She needed him, and he needed her. There was no other who could light his lips with a smile, fill his heart with joy, and gratify his soul with pride. Nothing made him prouder than when she sat curled up over her stomach and pushed with all her might.

He braced his arm across her back and coached her as Mara had instructed him. With each push, the baby was closer to delivery, and Gustaf encouraged the priest to speed it up. As the last words fell from the monk's lips, an infant's tiny cry broke through the commotion of the room. Æsa dropped to her back in exhaustion and Gustaf stared as Mara lifted the bloody little babe for him to see.

"A boy," Mara said tearfully. "My nephew. You did it, Æsa. You birthed a son."

Gustaf swiveled his head toward the priest. "Did you marry us?"

The monk smiled. "You're husband and wife in God's eyes. What God has joined, let no man tear asunder. And God help them if they do."

Gustaf wrapped his arms around Æsa's spent body and buried his face in her neck. "I love you, wife. I love you. Do you hear me?" He felt Æsa's hand on his cheek but heard nothing from her lips save for long, deep breaths.

"Do you want to hold your son, Gustaf?" Mara asked as she wrapped the wailing child in clean linen.

He looked at Æsa, then glanced at the infant with apprehension. "Hold him?"

Mara carried the child to him and helped fold Gustaf's arms in a cradle. She transferred the bundle into his embrace, praising him as he gentled the newborn in a slow rocking motion. The babe settled down and snuggled into place.

"See," Mara commended. "He knows who his father is already."

"You think so?"

"He feels safe enough to sleep." Mara ran her fingertips over his delicate forehead and returned to her place between Æsa's legs to tend to the afterbirth. "You can leave now, Father."

"Bless you, child." The priest scurried out the door, clearly desperate to forget the indecent position in which he'd seen Æsa.

Gustaf made the mistake of looking over at Mara. The copious amount of blood, flesh, and membranes she extracted from his wife unsettled his stomach. The vivid red stain of blood on the linens and Æsa's thighs pulled on his heartstrings.

Mara regarded his disconcerted reaction. "'Tis all right, Gustaf. Æsa feels no pain. I will have her cleaned up shortly."

Trusting in Mara, he forced his gaze to remain on the little one in his arms. From the tufts of reddish-blond hair on his son's head to the button nose above his full lips, he'd never seen such a beautiful sight. He glanced at Æsa only to find her staring at him, smiling.

"What shall we name him?" Æsa asked.

He laid their son next to her on the boxbed and drew his family together in his arms. "I think we should name him Dagr, after Dægan."

Mara looked up at Gustaf, and they exchanged an unspoken appreciation for what the other had done in this miraculous moment. Mara for helping bring his son into the world, and Gustaf for naming his son after her late beloved husband.

Æsa tested it on her lips. "Dagr, son of Gustaf, son of Rælik. It sounds perfect. Wouldn't you agree Mara?"

Mara wiped a tear with her sleeve. "I think 'tis a very noble name. Dægan would be proud." She stood to wash up and minutes later, she brought a package to Gustaf. "I was told by Jørgen to give this to you."

Gustaf sat up in surprise. "I nigh forgot about it. 'Tis a gift from Ulfr and Ketill. They gave it to me on the day we left with strict instructions not to open it until after the birth of our son," he explained to Æsa as he untied the crisscrossing of leather straps. He pulled out a thick cloak of deep brown bear fur and shook it out. "Ah, just as I suspected. Ulfr finished tanning the hide of the bear I slayed—as a gift. A wedding gift from me to you. What do you think?"

Æsa ran her hand down the soft sable fur. "'Tis beautiful. I shall wear it with pride.

As Gustaf spread it over his wife and child, another cloak of smaller size fell out. "Well, look at that. Little Dagr has his own cloak too." He draped the cloak over his son as Æsa cradled the newborn to her breast and nursed him.

His son was born. His Æsa was now his beloved wife. And his future had the potential to afford him a long life of happiness and harmony. He closed his eyes and savored the quiet reflections in a place he could call home—a home where all the descendants of Rælik could for evermore live in peace.

THE END

Author's Note

If you enjoyed *Tempered Steel*, I encourage you to try *Emerald Glory* (if you haven't already) so you can read about how Gustaf and Æsa first met.

Not only that, but you'll get acquainted with Gustaf's two younger brothers and the women who love them, for an epic tale of passion, betrayal, and redemption.

If you've already read all four books, then I can't thank you enough! Your dedication to finishing the series is appreciated more than you will ever know.

I'd love to hear from you! Feel free to send me a little note about what you thought of the series, if not just to say hello. I always love to keep in touch with my readers.

And lastly, I wanted to mention that I also write contemporary romance. I currently have two different series to choose from:

Jamett & Joseph Series
and the
Mavericks of Meeteetse Series.

I do hope you'll give them a try.

Sincerely yours,
Renee Vincent

If you enjoyed this book by Renee Vincent, please consider leaving an honest review at your favorite vendor. Reviews not only give credibility to an author's work, they also help other readers find quality books worth reading.

About Renee Vincent

RENEE VINCENT is a *USA Today* bestselling author of romance and women's fiction. Her books have earned numerous accolades, including a #1 Bestseller for Viking Romance.

She lives on a secluded hundred-acre horse farm in the rolling hills of Kentucky with her husband, two beautiful daughters, and a few fur babies who've managed to weasel their way into a couple of books. When she's not writing, she loves to decorate (and redecorate) her home, knit cozy blankets, send homemade cards to family and friends, and concoct her own versions of recipes to pass down to her girls.

Through the years, Renee has connected with some of the most dedicated and gracious readers who crave unpredictable plot twists, gripping adventure, and undying love. For that, she is most grateful.

www.ReneeVincent.com

Books By Series

Vikings of Honor Series
Sunset Fire, Book 1
Emerald Glory, Book 2
Souls Reborn, Book 3
Tempered Steel, Book 4

Mavericks of Meeteetse Series
Longing for Langston, Brody & Liv, Book 1
Made for McKinley, Jonas & Ava, Book 2
Falling For Forester, Cole & Crys, Book 3

Jamett & Joseph Series
The Start of Something Good, Book 1
The Road to Something Better, Book 2
The Gift of Something Grand, Book 3
Something's Bound to Happen, Books 1 – 3

Stand Alone Novel
Silent Partner

ReneeVincent.com